GUSTAV GLOOM

AND THE NIGHTMARE VAULT

by Adam-Troy Castro
illustrated by Kristen Margiotta

Grosset & Dunlap
An Imprint of Penguin Group (USA) Inc.

GROSSET & DUNLAP
Published by the Penguin Group
Penguin Group (USA) Inc., 375 Hudson Street, New York, New York 10014, USA
Penguin Group (Canada), 90 Eglinton Avenue East, Suite 700, Toronto, Ontario
M4P 2Y3, Canada (a division of Pearson Penguin Canada Inc.)
Penguin Books Ltd, 80 Strand, London WC2R 0RL, England
Penguin Ireland, 25 St Stephen's Green, Dublin 2, Ireland
(a division of Penguin Books Ltd)
Penguin Group (Australia), 707 Collins Street, Melbourne, Victoria 3008, Australia
(a division of Pearson Australia Group Pty Ltd)
Penguin Books India Pvt Ltd, 11 Community Centre, Panchsheel Park,
New Delhi—110 017, India
Penguin Group (NZ), 67 Apollo Drive, Rosedale, Auckland 0632, New Zealand
(a division of Pearson New Zealand Ltd)
Penguin Books (South Africa), Rosebank Office Park, 181 Jan Smuts Avenue,
Parktown North 2193, South Africa
Penguin China, B7 Jiaming Center, 27 East Third Ring Road North,
Chaoyang District, Beijing 100020, China

Penguin Books Ltd, Registered Offices: 80 Strand, London WC2R 0RL, England

Text copyright © 2013 Adam-Troy Castro. Illustrations copyright © 2013
Kristen Margiotta. All rights reserved. Published by Grosset & Dunlap, a division of
Penguin Young Readers Group, 345 Hudson Street, New York, New York 10014.
GROSSET & DUNLAP is a trademark of Penguin Group (USA) Inc.
Manufactured in China.

Book design by Christina Quintero. Typeset in MrsEaves, Neutraface, and
Strangelove Text.

Library of Congress Control Number: 2012012898

ISBN 978-0-448-45834-2   10 9 8 7 6 5 4 3 2 1

This one's for Gabriel, Julian, and Chance

CHAPTER ONE
GUSTAV MEETS FRIED CHICKEN

In the big front yard of a big black house, four people and a number of shadows sat down to what looked like the most ominous picnic in the world.

It was a friendly occasion that only looked ominous because of the dark gray cloud that always hung over the sprawling Gloom mansion, blocking out sunlight and giving an eerie cast to the yard, which was always covered with a thick layer of rolling gray mist. The only tree on the grounds was a brown, barren thing that looked exactly like a clutching hand reaching up out of the earth. It somehow looked even less cheerful with the child's swing that hung from one of the fingers.

Given a choice, most people would have moved the picnic to the yard of the Fluorescent Salmon house on the other side of Sunnyside

Terrace, where the lawn was green, there were no gray mists, and the sun shone like a jewel in the sky. But the strange young boy in the black suit didn't have a choice; he could not venture beyond his own front gate, so his new friends, the What family, had brought their folding tables and chairs, their picnic coolers, their checkered tablecloth, and their flying discs over to his place.

The result had been a perfectly acceptable picnic so far, even if the game of catch with the flying disc had ended unsatisfactorily when it suddenly disappeared in midtoss and didn't appear again for twenty minutes, finishing its flight when there was no longer anybody in place to catch it. Even Gustav had been unable to explain where it had been in the intervening time, though everybody noticed that it was now, somehow, half-melted.

"This," ten-year-old Fernie What said, "is fried chicken."

She served him a drumstick on a paper plate.

Gustav Gloom regarded her offering with deep suspicion. He had never eaten fried chicken. In fact, until two weeks ago, when

Fernie and her family brought freshly baked chocolate chip cookies to his fenced-in front yard, he had never actually eaten food.

Growing up in the big black house, Gustav had survived on the meals his shadow ate. It was shadow food and could not be eaten by human beings, but it had nourished Gustav for all his life without his ever eating a meal with his own mouth. This was an intolerable situation that the What family, including Fernie's twelve-year-old sister, Pearlie, and their father, Mr. What, had promised to correct.

Stalling, he asked, "Shouldn't I also get those things to eat with—what are they called again?"

"Utensils," Fernie said. "You'll get to use a fork in a little bit, for the coleslaw and macaroni salad. But most people don't use one for fried chicken. You're supposed to eat it with your hands."

Gustav appreciated any opportunity to show that he was paying attention. "Like that round thing you cut into slices a few days ago."

"Pizza," Pearlie said.

"Piece Of," Gustav recalled.

"No. *Pizza*." She spelled it: "*P-I-Z-Z-A*."

"Spelled that way, it should be pronounced *pizz-zzuh.*"

"Well, it's not," Pearlie said. "It's *pizza.*"

"Why can't we just have that again?"

"Because you can't have pizza for every meal," Fernie said, uncomfortably aware that it was the kind of thing a mom would have said. "This is fried chicken, one of my favorites. Just pick it up and eat the meat around the bone."

"Yes," said Mr. What. "Be careful with that bone. You don't want to choke on the bone."

This was a pretty typical thing for Mr. What to say. He was a professional safety expert and made his living teaching people how to avoid deadly accidents. Fried chicken was, in his view, so very dangerous that he'd written an entire book, *The Deadliest Cluck,* about the terrible catastrophes it could cause. According to the book, choking on a swallowed bone was not even the worst. Chapter 7 described one case where a woman had hiccuped at the wrong time and inhaled an entire chicken leg up her right nostril, then sneezed it out and shot her husband through the heart.

Mr. What knew almost every terrible thing that could possibly happen to people in any situation, but was adjusting to the special challenges that went along with living across the street from a house populated by shadows.

Gustav tore off a piece of dark meat with his teeth. He chewed, perked up, and swallowed. "You were right. This is really good. It may even be my new favorite food."

"See?" Fernie said. "I told you."

He examined the drumstick, which now had one bite removed. "And you say that this comes from a bird?"

"Well, yeah."

"That's pretty strange," Gustav said. "Doesn't the bird object?"

Fernie and Pearlie glanced at each other. "I guess it would," Fernie said finally, "if anybody asked it."

"What about pizza?" Gustav wanted to know. "Is that a bird, too?"

Fernie said, "It would be an awfully strange bird. Spinning through the air like a flying saucer and dropping tomato sauce and green peppers on people as it passed by."

"So," Gustav said, inevitably, "is it?"

"That would be neat," Pearlie mourned, "but no."

Gustav nodded and went back to attacking his chicken.

For Fernie, watching him eat was almost like tasting fried chicken for the first time herself. Gustav enjoyed it so much and would never have known it if he hadn't become such a good friend to the Whats in the three weeks since her family had moved in across the street.

In that time Fernie had experienced the discovery that shadows were alive; the revelation that the house across the street was one of only a few in the world with gateways to the Dark Country where shadows came from; the unsettling report that the Dark Country was home to an evil shadow named Lord Obsidian, who dreamed of conquest; and an introduction to this young boy raised by shadows who, for some reason not yet explained, couldn't ever leave his property without going up like a puff of smoke.

These were not things she'd ever expected to encounter, but they'd changed the way she looked at the world forever. Even when away from home, like on the day her father had dragged her to a nearby city for an exciting all-day symposium on safety railings, she hadn't been able to avoid noticing all the shadows drifting to and fro on their own important errands; some had even said hello, and only Fernie and her father had noticed.

A couple of days ago, she'd asked Gustav why she hadn't been able to notice them before. Gustav had explained to her that most people in the world of light made a habit of keeping themselves from noticing because it didn't make sense to anybody unless they already knew. Once people noticed, though (which they could hardly help doing once they'd gotten too close to the Gloom house), there was really no way of stopping themselves from noticing. It would be, he told her, a little like trying to have a conversation with somebody who had a bit of ink at the tip of her nose. As long as you didn't see that it was there, it wouldn't bother you. But once you've seen it, it's always there, and you just have to get used to it. (This had been as good an explanation as any, and not so incidentally was Gustav's gentle way of telling Fernie that she did, in fact, have a bit of ink at the tip of her nose.)

As Gustav started on his second piece, a pillar of gray-black darkness rose from the mist swirling around the table legs and said, "I must say, girls, it all looks terrific. I almost wish I could have some myself. But I'm afraid it would go straight to my hips."

This was Gustav's great-aunt Mellifluous, the elegant and somewhat overweight shadow of a Chicago woman now deceased, who was as close to an adoptive parent as Gustav had ever known. She was kidding, of course, as any solid food going in her mouth would have fallen through her before it ever got to her hips.

Gustav spoke through a mouth filled with chicken. "Why would it go to her hips?"

"Too much fried chicken can make you fat," Pearlie explained.

Gustav stopped chewing. "I thought too much of any kind of food could make you fat."

"Yes, but fried chicken does it faster."

He regarded his second piece of chicken with significant alarm. "How much faster?"

"It's not gonna happen in the time it takes you to finish that piece."

"So it's not like magic," Gustav confirmed. "No sudden 'Poof, you're fat'?"

"Nope. No sudden poof."

"Okay," he said, and went back to eating.

Grinning, Fernie got up and went to the cooler for a soda. It was a few steps from the site of the picnic table, and the gray-black mist swirled over the cuffs of her jeans as she knelt and checked out the flavors. They had grape (which she considered a fine fruit but a disgusting flavor of soda), orange (Pearlie's personal favorite, though Fernie considered it vile), and her father's favorite, Safety Cola (which had all the carbonation removed to make sure none got up somebody's nose and distracted him at a critical moment). Finally, she found a can of her own favorite, the cherry-flavored Bloodred Hungry Zombie Blood Fizz.

She only realized just how long she'd been kneeling in place, soda in hand, a sudden darkness shrouding her sun-freckled face, when Great-Aunt Mellifluous came up behind her and asked, "Are you all right, dear?"

"I'm just thinking."

Great-Aunt Mellifluous clucked in sympathy. "This *is* a strange front yard for someone raised in sunlight, isn't it?"

Fernie glanced back at the table to see if Gustav or her family could hear her; but no, he was back to his fried chicken and intent on some long and involved story Pearlie was telling. "I don't mind. It's just that—"

"What, dear?"

Fernie bit her lip and leaned in close. "Would it be okay if I spoke to you in private for a couple of minutes?"

"Of course, Fernie. You should never be afraid to talk to me. You're like family. Where would you like to go?"

"Maybe under the tree," Fernie said.

Closely followed by Great-Aunt Mellifluous, Fernie sat down on the little wooden swing that hung from the thumb of the Gloom yard's only tree. She gave the dust at her feet a few halfhearted kicks while gathering her thoughts.

After a second or two, she managed: "I keep thinking about everything Gustav's missing. There's so much to the world outside the fence. I mean, my mom's in Kenya swimming with crocodiles for one of her TV specials; she gets to go to interesting places and see interesting things *all the time*. My dad gets to go into the city for work, even if he only walks near tall buildings when he's sure that they have no open windows filing cabinets might fall from. But Gustav never gets to go anywhere. Everything else has to be brought to him, and that's *not fair*."

"Life isn't always fair, dear. At least it gives Gustav friends like you and Pearlie, who can do for him what he can't."

Fernie turned the swing in place two or three times, twisting the cords that bound it and her to the overhead thumb. "But that's the part I can't stop thinking about, Auntie. I mean, why can't he? I know that something bad must have happened to his flesh-and-blood family, if you had to adopt him. But how does that end with Gustav trapped here forever? When does that start making sense?"

For just a moment, deep sadness seemed to make Great-Aunt Mellifluous less transparent and more solid than the shadow she really was. "I'm sorry, Fernie. I know this is all still new and confusing to you, but you really aren't asking the right kinds of questions."

"Okay. So what are the right kinds of questions?"

"The real mystery," Great-Aunt Mellifluous said, "is not what happened to prevent Gustav from ever being able to survive outside the estate grounds, but what gives him life in the first place."

Fernie did not see this as helpful. She turned away and found herself watching an ice-cream truck with black windows as it passed down the street that separated Gustav's house from her own. It was the first time she'd seen this particular truck, with a big model of a strawberry cone affixed to its front grille. She had the same thought that always flitted across her mind whenever an ice-cream truck went by, namely that it would be nice to run out and have a sprinkle sandwich, but then she remembered that she was already at a picnic.

So she turned back to Great-Aunt Mellifluous, intent on suggesting a return to the table, but saw at once that something was terribly wrong.

It was impossible to say that the shadow woman had gone pale, because she was the same shade of see-through gray she always was, but she did look stricken, in the manner of a lady who has just seen the fin of a great white shark slicing the surface of her backyard pool. "Oh, dear."

"What's wrong?"

"I'm afraid you're going to have to forgive me," Great-Aunt Mellifluous said, her usually strong voice now weak and quivery, "but we'll have to postpone this conversation for a while, as I have to rush inside and take care of a few things. Is that all right?"

"Of course," Fernie said.

Great-Aunt Mellifluous glanced back at the picnic table. "You may finish your picnic with Gustav, but afterward you need to go straight home, and stay there the rest of the day and night. And promise me something, dear?"

"Sure. What?"

"Stay *away* from that ice-cream man. *Run* away from him if you have to. He's not what he looks like. He's something very, very bad."

As soon as she said this, Great-Aunt Mellifluous dissolved like a puff of smoke and joined the swirling cloud at her feet. But she wasn't the only thing that vanished. All over the Gloom yard, the mist started pulling back, a great gray tide that retreated from its comfortable coverage of every nook and cranny of the estate and hurried toward the mansion's opening front doors. It seemed intent on escape, driven by fear of whatever terrible thing Great-Aunt Mellifluous had seen.

As the last of the mist retreated inside the

house, the black grass of the lawn was left uncovered, a field of stubbly black needles that somehow looked exactly like the upright hair on Gustav's head.

Fernie's own shadow, which like all shadows all over the world had a mind of its own, stayed with her, but only just; the instant the shadow mist had disappeared, the shadow Fernie lay revealed at her feet, and took a few tentative steps toward the house before darting back and remaining, as if in defiance, at the feet of the girl who gave it form.

The ice-cream truck disappeared around the next corner, still jingling its bells and attracting absolutely no interest from anybody in the neighborhood. Fernie had the feeling that it would be back.

Over at the picnic table, Fernie's dad peered down at his feet, which were suddenly not shrouded by fog. "Hey, look! The weather's improving!"

Gustav looked down at his feet, too. "It's not weather. It's the shadows. They've all gone indoors for some reason. They must be having a family meeting of some kind."

"Does that happen a lot?" Pearlie asked.

"Enough." Gustav shrugged. "They get involved in a lot of political arguments, and sometimes call in reinforcements when one side is losing."

Fernie didn't see any reason to ruin his picnic, since he'd had so few during his strange life, so she returned to the table and pretended to be calm while the family finished the chicken and had watermelon slices for dessert.

But even as Pearlie taught Gustav to spit watermelon seeds, Fernie couldn't help but wonder: What about an ice-cream man could possibly be scary enough to frighten shadows?

And why was she so terribly afraid that she'd soon be finding out?

CHAPTER TWO
THE VERY IMPORTANT NEIGHBORHOOD MEETING ABOUT FINALLY DOING SOMETHING ABOUT YOU-KNOW-WHAT

Later that day, after the What family had returned home, Fernie retired to the living room and curled up with her black-and-white cat, Harrington, and an exciting new book about a pair of mummy-hunting archaeologists named Oozle and Boozle. But she was unable to concentrate on the story and drifted away around the time when the two explorers found themselves trapped in a crypt by millions of hungry beetles. She found herself staring out the window at the Gloom house. As always, it was big and black and ominous and clearly hiding any number of secrets.

The ice-cream truck drove by, jingling its happy tune—maybe the twentieth time she'd seen it pass or heard that tune in the last few hours. Each time the truck went by, she'd felt a deeper chill.

She said, "I don't know what that truck's selling, Harrington, but I don't want any."

Harrington, who had gone wide-eyed at the first sound of bells, hissed at the truck as it went by, itself an ominous sign, since cats have a special sensitivity to shadows and tend to feel bothered when they're up to no good. His plaintive meow when the truck passed out of sight again was Cat for "Why don't you do something about that scary thing?"

"There, there," Fernie said as she petted him. This was Little Girl for "I don't know what to do, but petting you makes me feel better."

Harrington purred. *Me too.*

The doorbell rang.

Fernie fit her feet into her new pair of slippers (the ones that looked like some bloodred mutated alien blob that had glommed itself around her feet and was now working its way up her ankles) and went to see who it was.

She and Harrington got to the door just behind Pearlie, who opened it.

"Hello," said Mrs. Adele Everwiner.

The What girls had been raised to show respect toward their elders, and for the most part obeyed that simple commandment, as it was generally easier to be nice than not-nice. But they'd both long since reached the age where it became obvious to them that some adults seemed determined to make that difficult.

Unfortunately, Mrs. Everwiner belonged to that category.

She was the kind of person who seemed to spend her life waiting for the precise moment when a visit from her was least wanted.

If you ever want to predict when a person like her is about to show up, then simply wait until you're comforting yourself with a thought like, *Well, at least Mrs. Everwiner isn't here,* and you can be assured of a knock on the door.

Both What girls managed a polite "Hello, Mrs. Everwiner" that sounded only a little bit less convincing than when they had looked at dinner and said, "Oh, great, spinach."

Their visitor looked like a human teardrop: wide and rounded at the bottom, narrower at her shoulders, and coming to a point on top. Her hair was as red as an apple and was the part that came to a point, even if the point was a little off center and leaned to the right, as if signaling to invisible people behind her that she was about to make a sudden turn. She had bright green eyes behind bright green eye shadow and a nose so small that it looked like it had been placed on her face as an afterthought.

Just below her shoulders she had affixed an adhesive sticker with the friendly words HELLO! MY NAME IS. Beneath that the sticker bore an empty space in which she'd handwritten *Mrs. Adele Everwiner, Founder and Vice President, Neighborhood Beautification Society*.

Reading it, Pearlie said, "Is *all of that* your name?"

Mrs. Everwiner glanced down at the sticker. "No, dear. I keep telling you, my *name* is only Mrs. Adele Everwiner. The rest is just my official title."

"Like lord or lady," Pearlie suggested.

"Or countess," Fernie added.

Mrs. Everwiner was such an important person in her own mind that she never saw when she was being messed with. "Except this is a democracy, dears. The Neighborhood Beautification Society doesn't go in for actual inherited titles."

"Oh, well," Fernie said. "As long as it's *official*."

"Thank you, dear. Hello, Mr. What."

Fernie's father had arrived at the front door. "Hello, Adele. What can I do for you this fine evening?"

"I just wanted to pick you up for the meeting," Mrs. Everwiner said, with a worried sideways glance at the girls. She leaned forward and whispered, "You know, the one about finally doing something about you-know-what?"

"Oh, yes," Mr. What said in a regular tone of voice, making absolutely no attempt at all to keep the matter the secret Mrs. Everwiner seemed to want it to be. "The very important neighborhood meeting about Finally Doing Something about You-Know-What. I'm sorry, Adele, I know that I promised to come, but the truth is that I forgot all about it."

"What's you-know-what?" Fernie asked.

Mr. What glanced at his daughter. "Adele here is launching another of her regular campaigns to get the city to condemn and tear down the Gloom place."

Mrs. Everwiner preened. "Somebody has to, dear. It's an *eyesore*. It doesn't fit the character of the neighborhood." This was her way of saying that, unlike the other houses on Sunnyside Terrace, it wasn't painted some headache-inducing color like Fluorescent Salmon or Radioactive Lime Green.

Mr. What said, "But it was here before the

rest of the neighborhood was built. Isn't the real problem that *they* don't fit in with *it*? Couldn't we solve the problem by just painting all the other houses black?"

"Sounds good to me," Pearlie declared. "I'll get the paint roller."

She actually turned around and started hurrying toward the closet, but Mrs. Everwiner called her back.

"That won't be necessary, thank goodness."

Pearlie stopped. "Why not?"

"We've found an old law in the city charter that empowers the authorities to demolish ugly buildings like that horrid Gloom place. The city can intervene whenever a majority of the residents within a two-block radius sign statements testifying to the aesthetic damage being done to the overall character of the surrounding neighborhood."

It took Mr. What a few seconds to put that together. "In other words," he said slowly, "you can ask the city to tear down any neighbor's house, as long as you can get enough of your other neighbors to gang up on them?"

"Exactly," Mrs. Everwiner said with considerable pride.

"But that's *not fair*," Fernie protested.

"Of course it's not," replied Mrs. Everwiner, who didn't seem to have any problem with that at all. "We do want to win, dear."

Pearlie asked the next logical question: "And what if the people living in a house you consider an eyesore don't want their home torn down?"

Mrs. Everwiner waved her hand dismissively. "Oh, the same law says that homeowners can get their houses ruled historical landmarks, or at least something called 'privileged prior construction,' that legally can't be torn down without the permission of the owners unless it's been declared unsafe. But in order to qualify for that, those owners have to file paperwork and talk to a judge. And nobody's seen Hans Gloom or any of his crazy relatives for years. Nobody even knows if they're still living there."

This was the very first time anybody in the What family had heard any reference to Gustav's non-shadow relatives. Fernie let it pass, and protested, "They've seen Gustav. He spends time in the yard almost every day."

"I know." Mrs. Everwiner sniffed. "But anybody with half a brain can tell that there's something terribly *strange* about that boy. If he were normal, he'd be going to school like other children. At least if we get his house torn down he can get taken away from those terrible people and put away someplace more *appropriate*."

Fernie was ready to cry that there was nothing wrong with being strange, and that Gustav didn't go to school because he couldn't, and that she'd rather live in the same neighborhood with him than with people who want to tear down houses, anyway.

But before she could speak, her dad suddenly made her very proud of him by saying, "Come to think of it, Adele, I believe that I will go to your silly meeting after all. Somebody has to stand up and tell you people what a completely cruel and inconsiderate idea you've had. Please go ahead, I'll be along in a few minutes."

Mrs. Everwiner was still sputtering when Mr. What closed the door.

Both girls cried, "Dad!"

He was at the front closet taking out the blue sweater he always wore when the temperature outside dipped below seventy. "What?"

The girls shouted together, "That was *awesome*!"

"No, it wasn't," he said. "It was rude. But

I've never had much patience for bullies." He donned the sweater, then picked up his umbrella and regarded it the way he usually did whenever weighing the chances of a sudden thunderstorm against all the possible freak accidents involving umbrellas and low-flying geese.

Fernie asked, "Can we come?"

"Not this time," he said. "I may have to use some strong language I don't want you to hear."

Pearlie said, "Come on, Dad. We read grown-up books. We have satellite TV. We learned all the bad words years ago."

"I know," he said regretfully, "but I'd rather not have either of you ever hear them coming from *me*."

He kissed them both good night, told them not to wait up, and placed Pearlie in charge before marching out the front door where Mrs. Everwiner still stood, frozen openmouthed at the moment the new neighbor had dared to shut the door on her.

Fernie almost wished she had a bugle she could use to sound a charge as he left his castle, intent on doing battle with dragons.

Outside, the ice-cream truck passed by one more time, and Harrington hissed.

CHAPTER THREE
WHILE MR. WHAT WAS OUT

Many people have had their lives saved by dogs.

Dogs are always dragging people out of deep water, standing between them and hungry bears, and racing over hill and dale to advise Mom that little Timmy's fallen into the well again.

A certain smaller number of people are saved by other animals.

Dolphins have been known to defend people from sharks, parrots have been known to dial 911, and at least one man we know about was *actually* saved from freezing to death by a pig.

Not many people are saved by cats.

This isn't because of any shortage of love in the feline heart, but because they usually sleep through most bad things that happen, or are too busy running away and saving themselves to worry much about saving anybody else.

Harrington was an exception, in that he had recently saved the What family and their new friend Gustav Gloom from a deadly killer known as the People Taker.

If you think he didn't remember that or constantly play back those events like a favorite movie in his little mind, then you don't understand cats or how much they like to believe that everything that ever happens in the world is all about them.

The drawback of all this was that Harrington also got to remember how many dangers lurked in the neighborhood. So while his favorite human being, Fernie, and his second-favorite human being, Pearlie, lay next to him on the living room couch that he permitted them to use, watching some pointless thing about little white objects zipping back and forth through space, firing beams of light at one another, he kept all his attention on the street outside, and on the house behind the black iron fence. He sensed that tonight the shadows were afraid, which disturbed him even more than the sound of a tuba. (And few things disturbed him more than the sound of a tuba.)

He wished he could consult with his own

shadow, which he sometimes chased and which sometimes chased him, but it was being exceptionally dull tonight, staying close to him and not doing anything that Harrington himself hadn't done. Harrington was smart enough to recognize this as a sign that it was also afraid; and that meant that he, also, knew enough to be afraid.

So he just kept watch while his favorite humans watched their stupid movie about little white darts zipping through space while shooting one another with beams of red light, and at long last, when it was past dark, his attention was rewarded.

He saw the ice-cream truck pull into the empty space in front of the What house and park.

He growled when the driver got out and stood in the center of the street, staring first at the Gloom house and then at the one where Harrington lived with his pet people.

He puffed his tail to three times its prior size when the driver finally turned toward the What house and began to march up the front walk.

He released a yowl as loud as anything that had ever emerged from his mouth.

Fernie said, "What's wrong, baby?" and happened to look up just as the yellowed and lumpy uniform of the ice-cream man passed out of the view of the living room window and onto the front steps.

She glanced at her cat and knew that whatever he'd just sensed was very, very wrong.

Then everything got real bad, real fast.

Just before the ominous knock she expected, Fernie cried out, "Don't let him in!"

Pearlie, whose hand was wrist-deep in a bowl of cinnamon popcorn, glanced up and managed to get out a single word, "Who?" before the door opened and the driver of the ice-cream truck walked in.

He shouldn't have been able to come in. Mr. What had locked the door when he left, and the girls had bolted it, according to his usual stringent safety procedures. A quick glance at the door itself, with its protruding bolt, and Fernie realized that it was somehow, impossibly, *still* locked, though the ice-cream man had just as impossibly managed to open it without splintering the door frame.

Pearlie stood up, spilling her bowl of popcorn on the floor as she angrily advanced on the intruder. "Who do you think you are, mister? This is a—"

Fernie yelled, *"Stay away from him, Pearlie!"*

Pearlie glanced back at Fernie and seemed to realize that her little sister knew more about this strange intruder than she did. She didn't advance any farther on the ice-cream man, who stood in the doorway, cocking his head from side to side as if he needed somebody to remind him what a living room was and what to do once he saw one. She just moved a little to her right, making sure that he wouldn't be able to get to Fernie without going through her first.

Fernie, who was just as protective toward Pearlie, got up from the couch and stood at her big sister's side, prepared to fight if necessary.

Even Harrington joined in, by puffing himself up as much as he could: a little cat making himself a somewhat bigger one, as befitted a beast who had once taken on a People Taker all by himself.

Pearlie spoke out of the right side of her mouth. "This is Gustav Stuff, isn't it?"

Fernie answered from the left side of hers. "I think so."

"Me too," Pearlie said glumly.

Gustav Stuff had become their private name for the strange and frightening things that sometimes happened in the vicinity of the Gloom house. This wasn't exactly fair to Gustav, but it was the phrase they had settled on.

The ice-cream man looked like Gustav Stuff. He was a squat, lumpy figure with no neck, a wide face with a mouth that seemed to stretch too far a distance between his baggy cheeks, and bright blue eyes that didn't seem to see the girls at all. He wore an all-white uniform with a cap, but his shirt and trousers weren't clean; they looked more yellow than white, almost as if they'd been white once but had been dirty for so long that the color had become part of the fabric.

He seemed to bring winter with him. It wasn't a crisp, comforting cold, either, not the kind that's fun in winter. It was the cold of something very, very wrong.

His baggy cheeks bulged and throbbed. "Interesting. It's just a house."

"It's not your house," Pearlie noted. "Get out and close the door behind you. You're letting in the bugs."

The ice-cream man seemed to notice that the door behind him was still open. He turned around and closed it. It shouldn't have been able to close with the bolt still sticking out, but the door shut with an audible *click*.

The cold got worse as he stared at them. He stepped out into the narrow tiled hallway between the living room and the kitchen, blocking their route to both the front door and the rear of the house.

Pearlie murmured, "Back door. First chance we get."

Fernie answered under her breath. "Race you there." Then she directed her next words, louder and more cheerful, to the ice-cream man. "Are you looking for something?"

He sniffed the air, rolling his strange, lumpy head from side to side as if trying to determine whether a tasty snack was being prepared in the kitchen. "I can smell it."

Pearlie sidled toward the picture window and closer to the ceramic sculpture on the little table next to the easy chair. "That's probably just the cat. It was Fernie's turn to scoop the box."

"Was not," Fernie said as she moved away from the window and closer to the sofa.

"No," he said, sniffing again. "Not the cat. I smell . . . shadows. *Fresh* shadows. *Many* shadows. You girls were inside the shadow house. You were *inside* and lived to see another day. The scent of the house is still on you."

"Well, I like *that*," Pearlie said as she inched still closer to the ceramic sculpture. "That was weeks ago, and I've taken something like twenty showers since then."

Fernie jumped up onto the sofa cushions. "I liked it better when I thought he was complaining about the cat."

Harrington's opinion of this, if he even heard it, went unrecorded. He hissed, but that probably wasn't meant for Fernie and Pearlie.

The ice-cream man's jaw fell open and for the first time revealed a formless darkness as black as anything Fernie had ever seen. Tendrils of black mist bubbled out between his lips. "October wants the Nightmare Vault."

"That's not even a sentence," Fernie noted.

"The Gloom house is too big for October to search by himself. There are too many rooms. But you were inside the house. You've seen things. You might know the Nightmare Vault. You might *lead* October to the Nightmare Vault."

Pearlie looked at her little sister. "Is he saying that October's his name?"

"Sounds like it. Why?"

"I'm just saying. The man's named after a month."

"That's not unusual," Fernie pointed out. "I have a friend named April."

"That's right," Pearlie admitted, as if remembering this for the first time. "And I know one named June. And Spider-Man has an Aunt May."

The stranger, whose lazy black gaze had shifted from one girl to the other throughout this conversation, as if truly hoping to find a helpful answer, now dragged himself back to his point. "You will take me to the Nightmare Vault."

Fernie bounced up and down on the sofa cushion, working up enough courage to run for it. "What do you think, Pearlie? Have any interest in doing that?"

"Nope," said Pearlie as she prepared to make her move. "I wouldn't give this guy directions to the nearest post office."

Then she lunged.

The ceramic sculpture was the single ugliest

furnishing in the family's possession. They actually called it "that ugly sculpture," as it had been given that very name by Mrs. What, who had been dismayed when Mr. What had bought it.

The ugly sculpture was a twisted green thing that looked like a stick of taffy some petulant child had given a half twist and then left to melt in the sun. It perpetually looked about to fall over, but stayed in place because the base was so heavy, the rest of it could afford to lean a little. Hideous as it was, the family felt a perverse affection for it, like they might have felt for a puppy that had managed to grow up and become an old dog without ever understanding why it shouldn't poop on the rug.

Pearlie grabbed the sculpture with both hands and drew it over her shoulder like a baseball bat.

October seemed wholly unworried that one of the girls had found herself a weapon. "You will bring me to the Nightmare Vault, or you will die."

"That's the first we've heard of it," Fernie told him. "You better leave and go look for it somewhere else."

His neck bulged, like a bullfrog's, and he staggered forward another step, looking less like a man walking on his own than a puppet being controlled by invisible strings. There was a powerful rumble, so low that it was hard to hear as an actual sound but so strong that the walls rattled and a set of glasses shattered in the sink.

Pearlie turned to Fernie and said, "I think this is it."

Fernie could feel the rumble on her skin, almost as if the entire house were an airplane and the vibration were the engines revving up enough power for a takeoff. "I think you're right."

Harrington yowled . . .

CHAPTER FOUR
THE MAN WHOSE MOUTH WAS BIGGER THAN HIS HEAD

October's mouth was not only bigger than it should have been, but bigger than it *could* have been—bigger, now, than his head.

His lips had opened up and folded out and peeled back in all four directions, making an opening that extended well above the top of his head and well below what should have been the base of his neck. They curled back until his mouth was big enough to swallow a manhole cover whole.

The inside of his mouth was a black emptiness uninterrupted by anything that normally would have been found inside a head.

The blackness began to erupt into the air around him in tendrils of nasty, grasping darkness.

Pearlie threw the ugly sculpture. It was much too heavy for her to throw very hard or very far, but shock and fear gave her strength greater than she normally would have had, and an accuracy that would have won her all the stuffed bears in every carnival midway that ever charged people a dollar a throw.

The ugly sculpture hit the circle of perfect darkness dead center, and then shrank rapidly as it gathered speed and tumbled into whatever bottomless universe existed inside October's mouth.

"Wow," Pearlie said.

It was about as respectful a *wow* as any she'd ever uttered.

The tendrils of darkness continued to spill from October's lips, twisting and curling and grasping as they made their way through the air and toward the two girls.

Backing up against the opposite wall, where her own shadow was scrabbling about looking for a way out, Pearlie said, "I'm out of ideas."

Fernie had nothing. Already the black tendrils stretched across the entire width of the living room, each one splitting into branches to create more, and still more erupting at every moment. They formed a kind of cage, closing the living room off from the rest of the house.

She supposed she could try to jump through one of the gaps between tendrils and knew that this was the best chance she'd ever have, as those gaps were already filling in, but it was impossible to know the right moment, and the prospect of picking one seemed more and more impossible the longer she waited.

Then Fernie felt something tug at her feet and looked down in panic, fearing it was one of the dark tendrils—but no, it was her own shadow, which seemed determined to shake her into action.

"Jump when I do!" her shadow said in a voice very much like her own.

Fernie yelled at Pearlie. "Here!"

"I see her! I'm coming!"

Pearlie and her shadow darted across the room, just barely dodging a grasping tendril that tried to loop around her as she went. They hopped up onto the sofa behind Fernie (and Harrington, who had also decided that this was the safest place to be) and waited the second it took for Fernie's shadow to make her move. They all ran when Fernie's shadow ran, using the sofa as a runway and leaping off the couch's last cushion just one step behind the helpful shape of the shadow girl who was showing them where to go.

The two sisters, two shadow girls, one cat, and one shadow cat succeeded in diving through a tiny gap between shadow tendrils, and landed in a pile in the hallway separating the kitchen from the living room. The two girls lay tangled there for a second or two, each one trying to be the helpful sister by pulling at the other to get up, while the panicking cat squirmed between them. For a few heartbeats that none of them could afford they pushed when they should have pulled and pulled when they should have pushed, and therefore remained a knot of tangled girl and cat.

"No, wait," Fernie said at the same time Pearlie said, "No, don't."

"No, don't," Fernie said at the same time Pearlie said, "No, wait."

Then each sister, talking to the other, said, "Quit it."

Harrington made an aggrieved sound that could have meant "Stupid people!"

They broke free of one another all at once. Harrington rocketed into one of the bedrooms, because the safest place any cat can think of is under a trusted bed. Fernie and Pearlie scrambled a little farther down the hallway on their hands and knees, even as October swiveled toward them and started to follow. Both could tell from the shifting shapes all around them that unless they moved fast, October would have them.

Then a voice that sounded just like Fernie's cried, *"No!"*

Fernie looked back over her shoulder. The shadow Fernie had been caught and was now furiously battling the long and whiplike tendril pulling her toward the ice-cream man's gaping mouth. She fought back as bravely as any shadow could have been expected to, so hard that she looked more solid than usual and no longer resembled a shadow girl, but rather a fuzzier, darker version of Fernie herself. But she was not as strong as the tendril that had grabbed her, and could not prevent her terrible fate. The shadow Pearlie hovered nearby, as if desperate to help, but could find no safe way to attack the ice-cream man on her shadow sister's behalf.

The shadow girl yelled, *"Go* already! He'll be after *you* next!"

The shadow Pearlie fled.

Fernie almost didn't. She almost *couldn't*.

Then Pearlie grabbed her by the wrist and yanked her to her feet.

Two girls and one shadow fled down the narrow hallway, racing past the open doors to the master bedroom, Pearlie's bedroom, and Fernie's own. The tendrils chasing them swept the walls of dozens of framed photos commemorating the best moments of the What family: the portraits of Fernie and Pearlie as babies, the picture of Mr. What in a tuxedo accepting the Morton J. Throckworthy International Award for Excellence for advancing the cause of protective safety railings, the one of Mrs. What in safari gear running away from an angry hippo. The sounds of breaking glass filled the air as the frames hit the floor, one after another.

Just as the two girls passed through the open door to the sunroom in the back of the house, Fernie happened to look back again and see her shadow being dragged into October's mouth. The shadow girl braced her shadowy hands and feet against the edges of his lips in a vain struggle to keep herself from being pulled in.

Fernie almost froze again. But Pearlie pulled her into the sunroom, a bright open space at the back of the house where a swinging window seat and a carpeted jungle gym for Harrington looked out upon a view that was a thin strip of lawn and a high wooden fence. It was a great place to sit if you wanted to bask in the setting sun while enjoying the picturesque view of a wall. All the two girls could see of the sky over that fence was a deep purple, just beginning to glow with stars.

The sight of Harrington's jungle gym, an elaborate arrangement of ledges and tunnels and dangling knots that he usually ignored completely in favor of the couch that was a lot less trouble, reminded Fernie that their beloved pet was still trapped behind them. "Harrington—"

"Is safe," Pearlie said, "as long as that guy keeps chasing us."

Fernie hated to leave her beloved cat behind but knew that Pearlie was right.

The girls reached the screen door just as October appeared at the entrance to the sunroom, his hands grasping the frame and his giant open mouth still giving off clouds of smoky darkness.

He said, "I want the Nightmare Vault."

"I know!" Pearlie cried. "We get it, already!"

A fresh wave of shadow tendrils swept toward the two sisters, who just barely managed to slam the back door behind them.

They poured on every ounce of speed they had as they fled along the fence and around the side of the house. The automatic safety lights Mr. What had installed on the roof clicked on as they ran by, bathing the girls in bright halogen light. Fernie could not help noting Pearlie's shadow, racing along the grass, even as her own remained missing, maybe lost forever. The absence of a shadow made her feel less real as a person, almost as if she were not part of the real world anymore. She couldn't help remembering the scary story Gustav had told her about Mr. Notes, a man who had been abandoned by his own shadow and was so traumatized by that loss that he now lived in a special home for people who had been rendered very twitchy.

The two girls crossed the street, ran past the fenced-in Gloom yard, and hunkered down behind a parked car belonging to a neighbor whom they sometimes said hello to and who struck them as either a secret agent or a dentist. Together they peered back at a home that was no longer safe for either one of them. It was impossible to tell from here that anything out of the ordinary was going on inside, but every patch of darkness the shining lights failed to reach felt like a possible hiding place for bad things.

Fernie said, "That guy just ate my shadow."

"I saw that," Pearlie whispered. "How did it feel?"

"I don't know. There aren't a whole lot of things in the world I can compare it to."

"Well, did it hurt?"

"It didn't feel like much of anything," Fernie whispered back, "but that's not the same thing as saying I'm okay with it. That was my shadow. I want her back."

The two girls thought they saw somebody and hunkered back down, pressing their backs against the dentist–secret agent's car.

Pearlie whispered, "Maybe you can borrow mine sometimes. So you don't look strange when you're out in the sun."

This was the kind of interesting suggestion that could only have been made by somebody who had been inside the Gloom house.

As much as Fernie appreciated her big sister's generous offer, she shook her head. "What are we going to do, take turns going outside? That'll be a fine thing on family trips to the beach. Besides, my shadow was a *person*. I've talked to her, and even been saved by her. It wasn't okay for her to be gobbled up."

Her voice broke a little at that last statement, and she came perilously close to crying, which would have been a very bad thing, because once she started, she probably would not have been able to stop.

Pearlie glanced over the hood of the car and said, "Look."

The automatic safety lights on the sides of the What house had just clicked off, leaving deeper patches of darkness that seemed too thick for a street with so many lights. Around the house, everywhere the shadows touched, the blackness swallowed everything. It was possible to believe that the one strip of darkness by the side of the house was not a lawn but a bottomless pit, ready to claim anybody who got too close.

Then edges of that darkness seemed to crawl, the black tendrils advancing like vines, too blind to see where the girls were but too stubborn to give up the search.

Then the outline of a man in a dingy white

uniform appeared, walking around the side of the house. The white uniform didn't seem very bright; it was just the suggestion of light, and the only reason October could be seen at all. The darkness, already impenetrable, seemed darker still where his head should have been.

"He's coming," Pearlie said.

CHAPTER FIVE
A GAME OF HIDE-AND-SHRIEK

October closed his mouth, though his face remained as lumpy and uneven as ever. He stopped in the center of the What lawn, throwing his head back so he could sniff the air. In the glow of the streetlights, the patches of darkness dancing around his head looked like a swarm of bees angry at being dipped in ink.

Pearlie whispered, "What are we going to do?"

Fernie understood that Pearlie wasn't really asking her. She was a big sister, and big sisters are always in charge, even when the little sister has spent a little more time dealing with scary monsters and knows more about what's involved. But only one decision made sense. "I have to go to the Gloom house and find Gustav."

"What could *Gustav* do?"

"I don't know," Fernie said with deep

irritation. "If I knew, I'd do it myself and save him the trouble."

Pearlie had to nod at the sense this made. "All right. So we'll find Gustav, and—"

As much as Fernie didn't want to be separated from her sister at a time like this, she could only shake her head. "No. You can't. Somebody has to stay behind and make sure that Dad doesn't try to come home while that guy's around. You have to go to Mrs. Everwiner's, yank him out of that stupid meeting, get him to a car, and have him drive away with you as fast as you can."

"What? Why?"

"Because he's covered with shadow-smell, too, and if he sticks around, October will go after him next."

October had followed the scent into the street and was now standing under the streetlight, sniffing the air again.

Brave as she was, Pearlie was unable to resist a little whimper. "But I'm older. I'm supposed to protect you. Why can't *I* get Gustav while *you* run away and warn Dad?"

This was the last argument Fernie wanted right now, but there was no way to get past it without first taking the time to have it. "Because

I've spent more time inside Gustav's house than you have. Because I know some of the dangerous places inside and might have a better chance of staying out of trouble. Because I probably have more shadow-smell on me than you do, and that means the ice-cream man's probably going to go after me, instead of you, if we split up. Because I can lead him away from you and Dad, and maybe toward something that can stop him."

Pearlie was being offered the easy way out, but she still shook her head, resisting the idea just a little bit more. "Dad's not going to go anywhere with you at Gustav's!"

"He has to," Fernie insisted. "And you have to say whatever it takes to make him. Tell him Gustav and his friends will help me. Tell him everything will be fixed by the time the two of you come back in the morning and that I'll tell him all about it over a nice waffle breakfast."

"You don't know that."

"If it's not all right by morning, it's never going to be."

Out in the street, the lumbering ice-cream man began to stride toward them.

The air grew colder the closer he came.

Pearlie only had enough time for one more

objection. "You'll be leading a man who eats shadows into a house filled with shadows."

"If he wants something in Gustav's house," Fernie said, "he'll be headed there sooner or later, anyway. At least now I'll be warning them."

Pearlie hesitated for one heartbeat more before throwing her arms around Fernie and squeezing her as tightly as she ever had. They'd always gotten along and had never suffered a shortage of sisterly hugs, but this particular hug was the kind sisters only give when they think it might be the last one ever.

Then Pearlie stepped out into the street and waved her hands over her head. "Yoo-hoo, you big smelly stupid-head! Anybody ever tell you that you have a *big mouth*?"

October turned to face Pearlie, his cheeks bulging and rippling enough to suggest snakes squirming around beneath them. "Yes."

Pearlie did a cartwheel, wobbled a little because she had never been all that good at those, and danced a silly butt-wiggling dance, as if this were all just one big joke and there was nothing else she'd rather do than make fun of the scary man with the mouth big enough to swallow ugly sculptures. "Well, I wouldn't mind your mouth being that big, as long as you did something about your *breath*!"

"I don't like rude girls," October said as he took his first step toward her.

Thinking her sister insane but also impossibly brave, Fernie took advantage of the distraction and sprinted to the front gate of the Gloom estate. It was closed, which she didn't see as a problem, because it was also usually unlocked. She pushed and found to her horror that this was not one of those times; whoever decided whether it should be locked or unlocked had figured on this being one of the nights when it should be locked.

It wasn't that big a problem, all in all, because one of Fernie's secrets—kept to herself because her father had a predictable list of terrible things that could happen to little girls who climbed things—was that she could climb trees and other things well enough to make squirrels jealous. She hopped up, grabbed the crossbar at the top of the gate, and in three short seconds pulled herself up.

Perched atop the fence, she saw Pearlie still taunting October with insults. He'd opened his mouth all the way again to release another torrent of shadow tendrils.

"Hey, you!" Fernie yelled, to return the favor and give Pearlie a chance to get away. "I know where the Nightmare Vault is—and I'm going to hide it where you'll never ever be able to find it, even if you look for a million years!"

October turned, the black hole of his mouth turning with him. Shadow tendrils exploded outward and began to grow in the air as he strode toward the gate.

Pearlie's fists went to her mouth at the moment the ice-cream man abandoned her to advance on her sister instead. A helpless apology flitted across her face just before she turned her back and began to run.

Fernie jumped down, rolled as she hit the black lawn of the Gloom estate, then scrambled back to her feet and ran for the mansion's pair of giant front doors. She found herself up against them, screaming for help and pounding on the wood with both fists, as behind her October reached the gate. He wrapped his pale, grubby hands against the iron bars.

Fernie wasted five full seconds hanging everything on the desperate hope that the gate would succeed in keeping him out, before remembering how easily he'd succeeded in opening and closing a locked and bolted door.

October pushed the gate open with no trouble at all.

"Oh no," Fernie said.

As October strolled through the open gate, the black tendrils from his mouth cut through the air like cracks in the world. They moved a lot faster than he did. In seconds there were so many of them, slicing the air between himself and Fernie, reaching out toward her like blind snakes, that there was no point in abandoning the Gloom house; those groping shapes would find her, wherever she ran and wherever she hid, even if she learned how to fly and soared to Liechtenstein.

She pounded on the door, screaming, "Gustav! I'm in trouble here!"

"Yes," October said. "You are."

The black tendrils were now fewer than three feet from Fernie, and she couldn't have run in another direction even if she'd wanted to; they'd formed a cage around the two front steps to the Gloom house and blocked every other possible direction.

"You should have cooperated," October said as the tendrils closed in.

Fernie pounded on the door. "Please, please, please! Somebody let me in! *I'm a friend of this house!*"

The doors opened.

Fernie, who'd been leaning against them with all her weight, fell flat on her belly. She landed on the long red carpet runner that extended down the long entrance hall to the grand parlor, dimly visible at the other end. The shadowy mist that should have covered the floor to ankle depth was missing. She saw nothing else between her and the rest of the house: no shadows, no Gustav, just the long hallway lined with tall vases and jet-black paintings.

Somehow, she managed to get to her feet and run, yelling, *"Gustav! Great-Aunt Mellifluous! Anybody! Help me!"*

As she ran, she reached out and toppled the giant vases, turning the hallway into an obstacle course that October would have to cross if he wanted to get to her. She heard the first and second and third ones all hit the floor with mighty crashes behind her as she ran, headed for the grand parlor and the escape it offered.

It was when she got to the grand parlor that she knew just how much the shadows feared the monster chasing her.

The first time she'd been here, the grand parlor had been a bustling, impossibly vast space, teeming with shadowy figures going about their shadowy business. There had been more of them than she could ever possibly count, gliding through the air, climbing and descending the multiple staircases, hanging out on the couches, and gathered in little knots of conversation everywhere the eye could see. Tonight, they were all gone. The grand parlor was just a room, abandoned by all the inhabitants, the scattered items of furniture as lonely against the great stretches of floor that surrounded them as empty life rafts on a vast, uncharted sea.

As she knew from her last visit, there were too many possible directions to run. She didn't have a clue where to go and where not to, which directions might offer help and which would only deliver her to worse danger. So she raced as far as the center of the forlorn and empty room and spun around, begging for some idea to occur to her. "Please, somebody! Gustav! *The ice-cream man is here!*"

Somewhere above her head, Gustav said, "So?"

CHAPTER SIX
THE ONLY THING THAT COULD HAVE POSSIBLY MADE GUSTAV'S HOUSE ANY STUPIDER

Peering down at her from the second-floor balcony, Gustav didn't seem particularly frightened, or even worried, just surprised to see Fernie.

He had changed into a different little black suit with a little black tie. Fernie could tell it was not the outfit he had worn earlier in the day, as that one had gotten some watermelon juice on the lapels, and this one looked like it had come straight from the dry cleaner. (This, of course, reopened the question of just who did Gustav's laundry, but that was something Fernie didn't have the time to worry about right now.)

Fernie found his look of only slightly confused calm infuriating. "Didn't you hear what I said? I'm being chased by the ice-cream man!"

"Oh," Gustav said. "You didn't say that he

was *chasing* you, only that he was *here*. *Chasing* you is something quite different."

Sometimes talking to Gustav made her want to stomp her foot. *"Are you going to pick on me or are you going to help?"*

"Help," Gustav decided. "Meet me at the top of the purple staircase, over there."

The grand parlor had a dozen staircases, including some that bypassed the second floor entirely and went straight to some of the upper levels. There were rickety wooden staircases and tightly wound spiral staircases, a few with missing steps, and one, leading to some high place obscured by haze, that only provided its users with one step out of every five, and therefore promised a painful plunge to the ground level for anybody who couldn't simply leap the yawning gap between boards. The purple staircase was one of the more regal, as it had ornately carved banisters, a plush runner, and a base that widened at the ground floor, as if to offer open arms to anybody who ever wanted to climb it. Fernie went for that one, her heart pounding as she took the steps three at a leap. Just as she reached the top she looked back and was driven to despair by the sight of October, entering the parlor with his mouth still yawning wide and a thicket of shadow tendrils invading the air before him.

Gustav met Fernie at the top of the stairs and was almost bowled over by the force of her grateful hug. As always, he showed only a limited understanding of what to do when being hugged, and demonstrated particular confusion over whether he should hug back. Looking over her shoulder at the new arrival, he said, "That doesn't look like an ice-cream man. That looks more like a shadow eater."

"He drives an ice-cream truck."

"Now I understand why you're so frightened by him; being chased by a regular old ice-cream man would be just plain silly."

Fernie couldn't help feeling that her friend was missing the big picture. "Would it really be too much trouble to hold *off* discussing what's silly and what's not until we *get away*?"

"Oh, not at all," said Gustav. "This way."

They rushed down the length of the second-floor balcony, the grand parlor to their right and a series of numbered doors to their left. Fernie couldn't help noticing that the doors ranged in design from polished mahogany masterpieces to featureless metal slabs, and that the room numbers weren't even close to being in sensible order, with one white door labeled ROOM 237, immediately followed by one dowdy green door labeled ROOM 101 and one bright red door labeled ROOM 3X2(9YZ)4A.

There was no time to worry about any of this, because the great empty parlor down below was filling up with the horrid black tendrils from October's mouth. Some were already more than halfway to the second floor, and would probably reach Fernie and Gustav in seconds.

The tips of those tendrils had just begun to poke through the empty spaces between the bars on the second-floor railing when Gustav skidded to a stop before a door reading ROOM 1 and wrapped his little fist around the jeweled doorknob. "In here!" he cried.

Fernie didn't have to wait for him to tell her twice. But she had been to Gustav's house before and knew that its many doors hid many sights as strange as the Gallery of Awkward Statues, as terrible as the Too Much Sitting Room, and as frightening as the basement level with a bottomless pit descending all the way to the Dark Country. So even as she followed him into a room so dark that she couldn't tell what it contained at all, a little part of her steeled herself for whatever strange sight might be waiting in there.

It turned out to be just a closet with another door on the other side.

Gustav opened that one and led Fernie into another closet that led to another that led to another that led to another.

Fernie could tell that they were putting some distance between themselves and October, because the unearthly cold he brought with him seemed to be going away. But after the ninth or tenth door, she still found herself getting exasperated. "I'm waiting for an explanation."

"For what?" Gustav asked as he led her into yet another small dark room with yet another identical door on the far wall.

"Why, out of all the other possible doors you could have picked, you picked the one that led to this."

One more closet and door later, Gustav said, "Why? What's wrong with this?"

"What's *right* with this?"

"Oh," Gustav explained as he led her into the latest closet in line, "this is a *very* useful place when you're being chased by a monster. It's always good to have a door between you and monsters. Two doors are better, three doors are better still, and five hundred doors are best of all. There were nights in the old days, when I was trying to stay ahead of the People Taker, when I put four or five thousand doors between myself and him, and didn't stop adding doors until I could hear him yelling, far behind me, that he was giving up for the night. He always got tired of it before I did."

"Unfortunately," Fernie pointed out, "you were so good at running away from him that you didn't get around to doing anything about him for months."

"That's true," Gustav had to admit.

Gustav led Fernie through another fifteen or sixteen doors.

"How long does this go on?" she demanded.

Gustav opened the next door in line. "Forever, I think. I always had to quit when I got hungry, but I've been told that if you packed enough provisions, you could keep going indefinitely."

As they walked through the next door after that, Fernie could imagine nothing so pointless. "What if you could pack provisions for a month? Or a year?"

"You do know what the word *forever* means, right?"

Another fifteen or sixteen doors later, Fernie decided that she had to be a little more aggressive about forcing Gustav to come up with a more helpful plan. "Isn't there some other safe place we could hide long enough to talk over what we're going to do?"

"We won't be able to stay there long," Gustav warned. "Those shadow tendrils have our scent by now and will be able to track us down if we spend too much time in one place."

"We'll wear ourselves down to nothing if we don't find somewhere we can figure out what to do."

Gustav surprised her by not arguing about it. "Okay."

He turned the next doorknob to the left instead of the right and they emerged into a well-lit, circular room with a high ceiling and walls bearing an array of lit torches. About twenty additional doors ringed the outer wall, each bearing the hand-painted words DO NOT ENTER ON PAIN OF DEATH! HORRIBLE,

Agonizing Fate Awaits All Who Venture Here! You Will Scream Forever Knowing You Disregarded This Warning and Met a Fate Worse than Death! This Means You!

Fernie had seen so many terrifying sights on her previous visit to the Gloom house that the prospect of any room horrifying enough to require such an earnest warning gave her chills. "Where are we?"

"The Choice of Horrible Fates Room," Gustav said. "Do you like it?"

She discovered that she couldn't tell the difference between the door they'd just come through and any of the others. "Right. This is *much* better than closets."

"You didn't say you wanted *better*," Gustav said. "You said you wanted a place where we could hide until we figured out what we were going to do."

She rubbed her forehead. "And once we do figure out what we're going to do, aren't we going to have to leave by one of those doors?"

"Sure," Gustav said.

"But those signs . . ."

"You like them? I painted them myself, when I was little."

Fernie looked closer at the hand-painted warnings, all of which persisted in looking ominous despite Gustav's reassurances. It may have been that the letters were all bloodred, and that they all dripped like blood, but maybe that was just the sloppy painting of a little kid. "So the rooms behind these signs are *not* dangerous?"

"Not all of them. One or two go to terrible places, but the rest are all safe. We're perfectly fine as long as we go through one of the safe ones."

Fernie was beginning to sense a big *but* coming up. "And you're about to tell me that you don't remember which doors are safe and which ones are dangerous."

Gustav looked a little embarrassed. "Right."

"Why didn't you just paint warnings on the dangerous ones?"

"That would have been a good idea," he admitted, "but I was bored that day and couldn't stop after only two."

Fernie folded her arms across her chest and gave Gustav the hardest look she could muster, which so unnerved him that he had to look down at his shoes.

"Gustav?" she said.

"What?"

"Remember that time I told you your house was stupid?"

"Yes."

"Well, it is stupid, and you just told me that you once did the only thing that could have possibly made it any stupider."

"I know." He sighed. "Every time I'm here, I could kick myself."

Fernie turned in circles and tried to figure out, just by looking, which doors promised safety and which hid fates worse than death. "So how are we supposed to pick a door and not get ourselves killed?"

"We don't," Gustav explained. "At least, not until we *need* to."

"Don't we need to *now*?"

"No. We just *want* to. It's kind of complicated, but the way it was explained to me, the Choice of Horrible Fates Room always lets you decide whether you want to be impatient and leave just because you *want* to, in which case you might pick a door that leads to something awful, or leave when you *need* to, in which case you'll almost certainly pick one that leads to the place you should go."

"So if we go before we have to," Fernie summarized, "we'll probably pick the door with the giant man-eating rat behind it, and if we wait until one of us really needs a bathroom, we'll probably pick the door that leads to one."

"See?" Gustav said encouragingly. "It's not so difficult, after all."

Sometimes talking to Gustav made Fernie wish for a handy cream pie to throw in his face. "Except that it wouldn't have to be even *this* difficult if your house didn't have so many rooms that led to horrible fates!"

Gustav was thunderstruck. "You mean your house doesn't?"

It wasn't Fernie's first reminder that Gustav hadn't ever experienced the world outside the Gloom estate, but it was one of the most maddening. "Of course it doesn't! Gustav, my house only has about ten doors in it, if you include the closets, and they always lead to the same places no matter how long you wait before opening them, and none of them lead to horrible fates no matter what you do!"

"Really?" Gustav asked. "Not even your front door?"

She started to say *Of course not*, but then shut

her mouth. Of course, he was right. All over the world, everybody's front door sometimes led to normal days and sometimes led to horrible fates, and there was never any way to tell whether it was going to lead to one or the other without walking through it and hoping for the best.

Maybe Gustav's house really didn't make any less sense than the rest of the world. Maybe it just made a different *kind* of sense: a mad, constantly changing sense that could actually be understood by somebody like Gustav who had spent enough time there.

So she calmed down a little. "So how long do we have to wait until we know we *need* to leave?"

"I don't know," Gustav said. "It could be a few minutes. It could be a few days. It could be forever. There was a skeleton on the floor the first time one of the shadows brought me here; I guess it belonged to somebody who missed his chance and never worked up the nerve to try any of the doors."

Fernie shuddered. "I'm glad you cleaned it up."

"So am I," he said seriously. "It wasn't the only skeleton I've found in this house, but the extra head on its shoulders was really creepy."

Fernie debated whether to devote any energy to exploring that, and decided not to. The Gloom house could be like that sometimes: so filled with strange sights and dark miracles and unanswerable questions that she had to let some things go unremarked in order to get on with whatever needed getting on with.

After a few seconds of hugging herself, wondering how Pearlie and her father were doing, and hoping that they hadn't mounted any efforts to rescue her, she glanced at Gustav again and saw him staring at her feet. "What?"

He had just noticed. "Your shadow's missing."

CHAPTER SEVEN
THE HOUSE INSIDE THE HOUSE

After all the fury and terror she'd been through, Fernie had almost forgotten. Now she felt a fresh wave of grief as she explained, "The ice-cream man ate her."

"Oh," he said, following that up with a heartfelt, "Yes. He does that. I'm sorry."

"Does that mean she's dead?"

"No. Shadows aren't really alive or dead the way people are; they're just things that exist, and don't bother with messy business like living or dying. I guess it's more accurate to say that she's been *collected*."

That didn't sound much better than being *eaten*. "What does he do with them after he collects them?"

"You saw those black snaky things that came out of his mouth? That's them, or at least the stuff they're made of. As long as even a part of them is inside him, they can't remember who they are, so they do what he wants . . . which is mostly collect more for his master, Lord Obsidian. You do remember Lord Obsidian, right?"

Fernie would always remember Lord Obsidian, even if she still hadn't experienced the displeasure of meeting him. He was a power-mad tyrant currently fighting a war to take over the Dark Country, who planned to conquer the world of people as well.

This was the first Fernie had heard about him snatching shadows. She'd known that he sent agents like the People Taker around the world to snatch human beings, but hadn't known that he made it his business to collect shadows as well. It was the kind of realization that left her wondering whether anybody, shadow or person, joined Lord Obsidian willingly, or whether they all had to be stuffed in sacks and forced to join his growing army against their will. Maybe the only way a fellow that awful could make friends was to kidnap some.

She glanced at Gustav's feet and noticed for the first time that he wasn't casting a shadow, either. "Where's yours?"

"With most of the others," he said. "Hiding in some corner where they hope the shadow eater can never find them. Some went down to the Dark Country, others took the portals to the world's other shadow houses, and others just found really, really good places to curl up and be quiet. It was a pretty rushed evacuation, so there must be a few in the more isolated parts of the house that didn't get the word . . . but they aren't any shadows you'd like to meet, I'll tell you that."

"Didn't they care that they were leaving you alone and defenseless?"

He looked sad. "Some did. Great-Aunt Mellifluous said that she'd take me with her if she could, but she had a responsibility to the others and was going somewhere even I couldn't follow. She had to be satisfied with telling me about the shadow eater and that I should stay away from him. My own shadow didn't want to leave me, but went along to protect her. Most of the rest—it's like I've told you: They may be the closest thing I have to a family, until I met yours, but most don't really have all that much to do with me. They ignore me, pretty much, and it's the same having them not here as it was having them here."

Fernie thought of the way she'd been forced to separate from Pearlie, not to mention her father, and felt a burning in the back of her eyes that she had to ignore in order to stay focused on the problem at hand. "And she didn't leave you with *any* idea of how to fight the shadow eater if you had to?"

"No."

"That's not very helpful," Fernie said.

"I know. I wish there were more, but it's not like there's any chance of your knowing any more than I do."

Fernie looked around the room and swept her gaze over each of the ominous doors in turn, imagining horrid fates behind each. She thought of something Gustav might not know. "He said he was looking for something called a Nightmare Vault."

Gustav made a face. "Ewww."

"Do you know what that is?"

"Sorry. That's the first I've heard of it."

"It sounds like it could be a bank safe or something."

"I know, but this house is full of strange things, and we could spend years just searching the rooms without ever knowing how to recognize a Nightmare Vault if we saw one."

She racked her brain for anything else the shadow eater might have said after breaking into her home . . . and for long seconds there didn't seem to be a single additional memory.

Then she remembered something else. "He also said his name was October."

Gustav froze. He was always a pale boy, but the sound of the shadow eater's name seemed to drain away what little color there was, as if the word itself were terrible enough to cut a hole in his heart. "October? Like the *month* October?"

The sudden devastation in his eyes frightened Fernie more than anything she'd ever seen or experienced in this house. "Yes. Why? What's wrong?"

The strange boy Fernie had met and had adventures with, whom she had come to consider the single coolest friend she'd ever had, and who had never betrayed a single moment of anger or despair while she was around to see it, did something she never would have expected from him: He cried out and threw a punch at the wall. His fist landed between two of the ominously labeled doors, and from the sound must have hurt his hand far more than it could have hurt the masonry. He held his injured hand in the other one, but was far from calmed; if anything, he seemed even angrier.

Fernie shouted. "Gustav!"

He seemed to notice her again, and said what might have been the worst thing he could have said with that expression on his face. "Thank you. I know where we need to go now."

He threw open the nearest door and plunged through into darkness.

Fernie was so concerned for Gustav that she didn't worry about the horrible fates that waited behind some of the room's doors. She just followed him through the opening into the next room, half expecting to immediately encounter the horrible fate that the warning signs on all the doors had promised.

Instead, she found the last thing she ever would have expected.

It was the opposite of everything she'd ever seen in her life, in that it was a room with a house in it.

The floor was a lawn. It was not real grass, but a lush carpet of some kind, with fibers that were just long enough and just verdant enough to mimic grass. Little yellow fluff balls at the tips of longer strands stood up here and there, imitating wildflowers. The ceiling and the walls to her left and right were a shade of blue exactly the same as a bright summer sky, complete with painted puffs of cloud to complete the illusion. Near the baseboards the walls became a mural of sprawling farmland, with a herd of black-and-white cows, white picket fences, and even a faraway lazy river, snaking in and out of some gentle hills as if in no particular hurry to get there and not in any way concerned that somebody might criticize it for its lack of ambition.

The sky even had a sun of sorts. It wasn't a real sun—at least, Fernie hoped not—but it was a ball of blazing fire, hanging so low in the sky that most household stepladders would have been tall enough to allow a tall man to reach it. It gave off more daylight than heat, but even so, the air had the comforting warmth of a beautiful morning in July.

The far wall was the front of a white clapboard house, with a screened-in porch and a pair of side-by-side rocking chairs looking out at the view of the fake lawn. On the second floor, below the place where the two sloping sides of the roof peaked, a round window made up of four panes revealed a ceiling painted the same shade of blue as the fake sky outside, and a dangling mobile with toy biplanes and rocket ships.

Fernie was just in time to see both the screen door leading to the porch and the wooden door leading to the house slam shut, one after the other.

She said, "Gustav?"

He didn't answer.

She approached the house with caution. It looked like any other inviting old country house, certainly more friendly in appearance than the larger house that contained it, but she had spent enough time traveling the dark passages and hidden rooms of Gustav's strange home to know that many things that looked harmless might be very, very dangerous.

When she reached the screen door, she opened it as if expecting it to bite her, and was only slightly encouraged when it didn't. She stepped onto the porch, the wooden slats of the floor creaking beneath her feet. She stopped halfway to the front door because she wanted to make sure that she really had felt what she thought she'd felt: a cool breeze, blowing through the screen around the porch and filling the air with the welcome scent of fresh air and newly cut grass. It was so real to her nose that she could almost believe that the house inside the house was really standing outside, in some nice place in farm country.

She walked through the inner door and into the front hall of a cozy family house. To her left was a dining room with a long polished table and enough seating for ten; to her right was a living room with couches, a fireplace, and a wall of books. In front of her was a long hallway leading to an open kitchen alongside a narrow staircase leading up.

She called again: "Gustav?"

Again, he didn't answer.

Fernie was not ready to climb that staircase yet, not without permission. She'd seen too many scary movies about girls who walk into abandoned houses and, like idiots, climb staircases leading to floors where some awful monsters lie in wait, eager to pounce on them.

The only thing *stupider* than climbing those stairs, Fernie believed, would be to go poking around in the basement, where there would almost *certainly* be a slavering monster who ate people. Or, if not a monster, then at least spiders.

She entered the living room, noting as she did that the windows all looked out upon what seemed to be green countryside, but which any close look revealed to be nothing more than a painted backdrop, the kind of thing she would have expected to find behind a window in a stage play.

"Gustav!" she called again.

There was still no answer.

Unsure what she should be doing, she approached the bookcase, mostly because she had never spotted a bookcase inside somebody's home without immediately taking a closer look to see what books the owners had been reading. She found a complete Shakespeare, a collected Charles Dickens, a book by someone named Shirley Jackson called *The Haunting of Hill House*, a few others she recognized, and on the top shelf a row of hardcover books with scarlet dust jackets. She picked up one of those and glanced at the title.

It was called *Beyond the Veil*, by Dr. Lemuel Gloom, PhD.

"Gustav!" she yelled. "Who's Lemuel Gloom?"

He didn't answer.

Fernie flipped the pages and turned to the back cover, which had a few words about the author beneath a big picture of his face. *Lemuel Gloom,* she read, *is an award-winning physicist, infamous for his controversial theories about worlds beyond our own. He is most notorious for his beliefs in the secret nature of shadows. Born in Liechtenstein, Dr. Gloom now lives in America with his wife, Magda, and his young son, Hans.*

Lemuel Gloom had a shiny bald head and a red beard that flared to white points at both sides of his mouth. He looked like a silly man, though possibly a friendly one.

Fernie flipped through the pages. The book was filled with strange charts and complicated equations. Fernie had always been a strong reader, but the one long sentence she started reading at the beginning of one chapter lost her after about seven words. It extended well past the bottom of the page and was still going strong at the end of the two-page spread after that.

A sentence like that contained either a lot of information or a lot of wind, and she didn't have the time right now for either. She returned the book, turned her back on the bookcase, and went to look at the framed photos on the wall.

They all depicted the same young couple, a pretty blond woman with bright hazel eyes and a man with a hawk nose and a smile that suggested he saw something funny he wouldn't mention out of politeness. There were photos of them wearing safari gear with thick jungle all around them, grinning at the camera while skydiving, standing on the tops of snowcapped mountains, and kayaking through white-water rapids.

It did not escape Fernie that these were all things her own adventurer of a mother did on a regular basis, and that she would someday like to do herself. She couldn't help thinking, just from the photos, that her mother would have liked the couple quite a bit . . . and discovered, thinking about it, that knowing them only from the photos, she liked them quite a bit as well.

The woman smiled in all of the photos except for one, where she was bent over some tropical fern looking at the single biggest spider Fernie had ever seen. Not counting the legs, it was almost as big as Fernie's closed fist. Fernie wouldn't have smiled at that spider, either, but she also wouldn't have leaned in close to it long enough to have her picture taken. The woman in the picture seemed to be frowning out of intense interest rather than the disgust any reasonable person would have shown upon finding a spider as big as a kitten. But that was not even the interesting part to Fernie; the interesting part was that, when there was no smile lighting up her face, she happened to look almost exactly like Gustav.

"Her name was Penelope," Gustav said.

Fernie jumped. She hadn't heard Gustav walking up behind her.

"She called herself Penny for short," he continued. "His name was Hans. He couldn't come up with a nickname shorter than that."

Gustav was always so serious about everything that the neighbors who spotted him in his estate's yard believed him to be the saddest little boy in the world. Fernie had learned that he wasn't as sad as he looked; he just didn't smile much. But sometimes he was sad, and he looked very sad indeed right now, the kind of sad that came from losing something very important, or from never having had it at all.

He carried a framed photo. "She would have been my mom."

She remembered the bio on the back of

Lemuel Gloom's book. "And Hans would have been your dad?"

"Hans was my dad," Gustav said. "Penny was never my mom. Somebody else had to be. But she *would have been*."

"I'm sorry, Gustav. I don't understand. Even if you're saying she died, she was either your mom or she wasn't."

"She did die," Gustav said. "But she never got to be my mom."

"But what does that mean?"

"It means she never had a chance."

He was so bereft, and so angry, that Fernie found herself a little afraid of him. "What happened?"

He handed her the picture in his hands. "*He* happened."

The three people in the photo stood in front of the Gloom house, looking like any other best friends happy to have their picture taken together. Two of them were the man and woman adventurers in all the other pictures. The woman looked heavier than she did in any of the other photos; she wore a T-shirt bearing the word *BABY* with an arrow pointing at her tummy. Her smile was golden. The man's was a little more crooked, but he still looked as happy as any man could be.

The other man with them was an older, paler figure with bright blue eyes, a high forehead, and a smile that suggested that he wasn't very good at smiling but was just doing it because it was expected of him.

He was not nearly as lumpy as the ice-cream man she knew, and his head was high and thin instead of round and misshapen, but Fernie recognized him, anyway.

It was October.

CHAPTER EIGHT
THE WORDS OCTOBER HEARD

"Is this the man you saw?" Gustav demanded.

Fernie, who was still a little frightened by the pain in the eyes of this strange boy she'd come to care about, needed a few seconds to find her voice. "It could be. The man in the picture has a normal head, and he doesn't look like he could open his mouth as much as October can . . . but yes, I think this is a picture of the person October used to be."

Gustav walked away, his shoulders shaking, and for long seconds stared out the window, as if seeing something beyond the fake horizon.

She took a step toward him.

Before she could even get close, he flung the photo out the nearest window. There was no glass in the window, so the only thing that shattered was the glass in the picture frame when it hit the fake blue sky outside.

He didn't turn around. "Before I was seven years old," he said, "I thought they were just on a long trip somewhere and would be back someday. Then I was old enough to hear the truth, and see that picture for the first time. He's the one who killed my parents. He's the one who made sure I became what I am. He's the one who made sure I could never go past the fence and know the world you know. It was all him."

Fernie drew close. "He doesn't look like he was a shadow eater then."

"No, not then. He was just a man. His full name was Howard Philip October. He wrote the same kind of books my grandfather Lemuel wrote, about ancient civilizations and evil spirits and elder gods and gateways to other worlds . . . the difference being that my grandfather actually made contact with the world of shadows, while Howard Philip October mostly just made up crazy stuff and claimed that he found it in lost ancient texts."

Fernie struggled to keep up. "Where was he supposed to get lost ancient texts?"

"From what I've been able to put together, he just said 'lost ancient libraries.' And if you asked him where he found the ancient libraries, he'd say 'the lost cities of lost ancient civilizations.' If you asked him where he found those lost cities and lost civilizations, he claimed to have found 'ancient lost continents at the center of the Earth,' but not many people went that far; you only have to ask that kind of question a couple of times to know the type of answer you're always going to get."

Fernie recognized this as the kind of answer that translated to "Because I said so," one she'd never accepted as the response to any tough question, not even from her dad. "Okay," she said. "And your mom and dad—"

"My dad," Gustav said with an odd emphasis, "and the woman who *would have been* my mom."

Fernie didn't completely understand why Gustav was so insistent on the difference. "Okay. How did they know him?"

Gustav sighed, stepped away from the window, and sat on the edge of the couch, his hands clasped between his knees. "My father grew up here, living with the shadows and every other strange thing my grandfather invited into the house, and though he was used to all of it, decided that he didn't want to spend his life locked up inside a dusty old mansion chasing other worlds all the time. He wanted to live a normal life, living in the world beyond the gate.

"So he left home, met and married the woman who *would have been* my mom, and for a few years traveled the world with her, never knowing when they returned for Grandpa Lemuel's funeral that Grandpa had met October and considered him a dangerous man."

"How do *you* know all this," Fernie wanted to know, "if it happened before you were born?"

Gustav looked at his hands. "I was told. In this room."

"By who? Great-Aunt Mellifluous?"

"No. Not her."

"Then who?"

Gustav opened his mouth to answer and then fell back into an unhappy silence.

Sometimes, a terrible secret can be even bigger than the hole it leaves in the story around it. The identity of the person who had told Gustav about his parents—or rather, his dad and what he called the woman who *would have been* his mom—seemed like one of those secrets.

Fernie sat down beside him, saying, "It's okay. Just tell me the parts you can talk about."

He nodded gratefully and moved on: "My father inherited the house, and Howard Philip October got in touch with him, saying, 'Hey, as long as you're not using the place, can I stay there for a while?' And my dad and the woman who *would have been* my mom flew home, met with October, and decided that he seemed like a good man and that it wouldn't do any harm."

"Of course," Fernie noted, "it might not have been easy for them to tell, since he wouldn't have been a shadow eater yet."

"No," Gustav said, "he wasn't a shadow eater yet, though he was already an ice-cream man, in a way, since his own family fortune comes from a company with a line of ice-cream trucks. I didn't know until now that he was the shadow eater, but it kind of makes sense that as long as he had to become a monster, he would still take a form that was familiar to him."

He stared at his hands some more and said, "The point is that my dad and the woman who *would have been* my mom—"

Fernie didn't think she could stand to hear that terrible phrase spoken one more time. "Why don't you just call her Penny? It's faster."

Gustav thought about it for a moment. "All

right. That works." He took a deep breath. "My dad and *Penny* let Howard Philip October use the house for a couple of years, while they were out in the world doing other stuff. They visited from time to time, to see how he was getting on, and after a while came to think of him as a friend."

He took another deep breath.

"And then, one day," he said, "they found out that they were going to have me."

The way he said it, you'd think they'd received some terrible mortal news, like the diagnosis of a fatal disease. He stood up and circled the room twice, as if there was so much anger attached to that part of his story that pacing was the only way to get past it without exploding.

Wanting to make him feel better, Fernie said, "That must have made them very happy, Gustav."

"I'm sure it did," Gustav said, in the tone of a boy who believed that they would have been mistaken to feel that way. "Nobody's ever bothered to tell me that part of the story, but I'm sure they took the news the way moms and dads are supposed to. I'm sure that if they decided to settle down anywhere else, it would have been as happy a thing as they wanted it to be, and I would now be a normal kid with a normal family like yours."

Fernie refrained from pointing out that a mom who traveled all over the world having adventures and a dad who knew all the ways people had been seriously injured by pencil erasers didn't make hers fit anybody's definition of a normal family. She guessed, "But instead they came back here to live."

"Yes," he said, and then repeated the single word: *"Here."*

She looked around at the room, with all its pictures of the happy young couple, all the little souvenirs and knickknacks on the shelves. And suddenly, feeling stupid for having taken so long to figure it out, she understood the importance of this place to Gustav's life. *"Here,"* she said. "In the house inside the house."

"Yes," Gustav said forlornly.

Fernie felt a chill. It was already noticeably colder in the house than it had been only a few minutes earlier, maybe a sign that the shadow eater was drawing close.

"Why would they move here? I thought you said your dad wanted a normal life."

"He did," Gustav said, "but from what I understand, the two of them weren't planning to stay here forever, just for a few months while they looked for a normal place to live. It was his own childhood home; he didn't think staying here for a little while would be a bad thing. Especially since he and Penny had *this* house, the house inside the house, to stay in while they waited."

She scratched her head. "That's another thing. Why would there even be a house inside the house?"

He sighed. "Because you've seen how endless the big house is. It goes on forever; it's so big that you could never explore it all, not even if you had an army marching down every hallway and knocking on every door."

Fernie had gotten that impression. "So?"

"Well, it's worse now that it's a shadow house, but it was pretty big even when it was only an ordinary house. It wasn't nearly as big on the inside as it is now, but even *before* Grandpa Lemuel made his deal with the shadows, even *before* the inside filled up with shadow-stuff and became so much larger than any ordinary house could ever be, the Gloom house was a great big sprawling mansion and the kind of place that would have been much too big for one husband and one wife, since it was originally built when the family was much larger and had enough room to house cousins, second cousins, third and fourth cousins, entire branches of the family nobody ever bothered to speak to, and I-don't-know aunts."

"What's an I-don't-know aunt?"

"Everybody has an I-don't-know aunt," Gustav said. "They're related to you in some way, but if you're ever asked to explain how, you have to say 'I don't know.'"

Fernie had to admit to herself that, yes, she did have several I-don't-know aunts, most of whom she saw just often enough to make it embarrassing to keep forgetting exactly who they were. "All right. So it was a big house. And . . ."

Gustav said, "It was too much house for Grandpa Lemuel, when most of the family had moved out and he was a young man married to my grandmother and raising my dad. It didn't feel cozy enough to him. So he built this house inside the house for his family, and they spent most of their time here. When he gave the rest of the big house to the shadows, he still kept this room with the smaller house for himself, so he could take a break from the shadows and everything they were whenever he wanted."

Fernie supposed that made sense, in the same way that anything crazy makes sense when you're living with the craziness. She said, "Okay. So when your dad and your mom—"

"The woman who *would have been* my mom," Gustav said, reminding her that he wouldn't give ground on this particular point.

"When your dad and Penny came back here to have you, they weren't interested in getting the rest of the house back, or interfering with whatever October was doing; they just wanted to stay in this small part of it for a while."

Gustav nodded. "They were friendly about it. They invited him to come over from whatever part of the house he was spending time in, to eat dinner with them every night. They practically made him a member of the family.

"But they'd been away for a couple of years by that point, and didn't know that he'd come to consider the Gloom house his own and resented their being back. From what I was told, he was also deathly afraid that they'd get around to asking him what he'd been doing all this time . . . and he was secretly working on a project so evil that if they ever did find out, they'd throw him out of the big house forever and never let him back in.

"Before long, it wasn't just a matter of pretending to be their friend. It was a matter of pretending that he didn't hate and fear them enough to want them dead.

"But even then, they might have survived knowing him. Even then, it might have been all right if they'd just moved out when the house being built across town was finished."

He sighed, and looked more miserable than Fernie had ever seen him. She realized that, despite the habitual serious expression that made so many people consider him the saddest little boy in the world, his usual intense interest in everything amounted to a kind of enthusiasm. It was an awful thing to miss when he was telling a story that gave him less reason for enthusiasm with every sentence.

He said, "Then one day Penny surprised my father with a decision. She said that she'd been thinking about it and that it wasn't so important to live in a normal house after all. She said that normal was overrated, and that people who open their hearts to different experiences get to enjoy life more than people who just want to be the same as everybody else. She said that as long as their child got to go outside and enjoy the sunshine and spend time with other children and grow up to be whatever he wanted to be in life, she would be proud to raise him in the house inside the house; and that she was sure he'd be all right, because my father had grown up there, too, and he was the best man she'd ever known.

"I've been told that he kissed her and told her that if this was what she wanted, then it was what she would have."

He took a final deep breath and spoke the next words all in a rush.

"Unfortunately, they had this conversation in the kitchen, on one of those nights when their good friend October was over for dinner. They thought he was on the living room couch. They didn't know that he'd gotten up and headed toward the kitchen to refill his glass of wine . . . or that he'd stopped right outside the door and heard everything they'd just said to each other. Neither one knew that he was their enemy, and that this was the very worst thing they could have said in his hearing.

"One week later, the woman who *would have been* my mother was dead."

He looked down at the floor and stared at it for a long time.

Fernie had no idea what to say, and like most people who have no idea what to say, said the right thing. "They must have loved each other very much."

Gustav looked up, his eyes red, even though he hadn't shed any tears. "Yes," he said. "That's what I've been told."

He almost said more, but then came to a decision and stood. "I don't think we have much time left," he said. "He'll find us soon. But there's still something else you have to see."

He headed for the hallway.

Fernie saw him turn at the stairway, glance at her, and start heading up.

She hesitated. She didn't know why, but she had the impression that whatever he wanted to show her up there was the worst part yet. She found herself afraid, for him and for herself, of whatever it might be. She also found herself wanting to turn her back and run, find her way out of the house, and never find out what it was.

One thing made that impossible. Gustav was her friend.

She got up and followed him to the second floor of the house inside the house.

CHAPTER NINE
THE PROPER USE OF THE WORD *SMELLY*

There were no horrible monsters at the top of the stairs, but there was something much worse, something so obvious that Fernie sensed it almost as soon as she reached the second floor.

It took her a second to recognize it as sadness.

The air on the second floor of the house inside the house tasted entirely different from the air downstairs. It felt, or tasted, or at the very least *smelled*, like a place where somebody who had once hoped for a happy future had lost everything and had been reduced to sitting by himself, thinking about what might have been.

A short hallway alongside the stairs led to three rooms, one in the front of the house and one in the back, with an open bathroom door midway between them. She couldn't see where Gustav had gone, so she checked the room in the front first. It turned out to be a baby's room, with a sweet little crib, a changing table, and walls painted the same gentle shade of blue as the fake sky outside. The same mobile with rocket ships and biplanes that she had seen through the window when approaching the house from the front yard hung over the crib, spinning slowly.

Nothing in it looked real to her. It looked a little like a cartoon, all outlines and bright colors, and she had trouble figuring out why until she realized that there wasn't a single shadow in it, not even where shadows should have been cast by the fake sunlight coming through the window.

Fernie had never realized before how much shadows help solid objects look real. She found that interesting until she remembered that she didn't have a shadow anymore, and then found it very frightening. Was the same true of her now? With her shadow gone, would people always look at her and think she wasn't quite real?

Something else bothered her as she glanced out the window. Despite that bright sunlight, the yard looked darker somehow. A pale mist, not shadow-stuff but the fog that forms on a cold morning, rolled across the fake grass. A thin layer of frost had formed on the fake flowers.

Gustav was right. It could not be long before October found this place.

Somewhere in the back of the house, Gustav said, "I'm over here."

Fernie left the baby's room, passed the bathroom, and went to the room in the back, which turned out to be the master bedroom.

Gustav stood just inside the door, his arms at his sides. "This was their room."

Fernie entered. Most of the furnishings were exactly what she would have expected to find in such a place, including the king-sized bed, a beautiful antique chest of drawers, end tables, lamps, a painted portrait of Hans and Penny Gloom at their wedding, and even a smaller bookcase lined with dog-eared paperbacks. There was no closet, but there was a freestanding wardrobe for hanging clothes, its doors open and all its contents removed. The door to the master bath led to exactly what it was supposed to. Everything looked bright and clean, just as if the family living here had moved out only yesterday. The view outside the windows was the same rolling countryside and the same blue sky she had seen through all the other windows.

But it was a strange place in other ways. From what she could tell, the mattress looked normal enough, but it was almost ten feet off the floor and rested on a wooden platform so massive that a ladder was built into its side to help whomever may have wanted to sleep there. Maybe it was a special kind of bunk bed, designed to reflect the fact that nobody ever wants to sleep on the bottom mattress—but there wasn't even space for a bottom mattress, just the platform itself. The end tables were on stilts to bring them to bedside level; one was covered with the remains of white candles, melted to nubs. Fernie saw the edge of a big book poking over the side.

She gave Gustav the kind of look she always gave him just before telling him that his house was stupid. "Why did their bed have to be so high up?"

He gave her the same kind of look. "They lived in a little house inside a bigger house, and that's what you find strange?"

She wilted. "It's just . . . it seems like the kind of strangeness that doesn't have a point."

"Lots of strangeness doesn't have a point," Gustav pointed out. "That's why it's called strangeness."

Fernie had to admit to herself that this made as

much sense as anything else she'd encountered in the Gloom house.

He said, "Stay here," climbed the ladder up to the bed, grabbed the book, and brought it back down to her. "This was their photo album. Most of it is pictures from their life together, but my father lived long enough to add a clipping from the morning after she died."

He put the book in her hands and turned to a page that he must have known well, because he found it without looking. The item he wanted to show her wasn't pasted to the page like all the happy photos preceding it, just folded up and tucked in the book, like something that had been forgotten there. It was a yellowing newspaper story, with a picture of Penny Gloom's smiling face under the headline: LOCAL WOMAN, 27, DIES IN WRECK ON DEAD MAN'S CURVE.

Fernie's heart broke a little. "Oh, Gustav—"

"You already know that she died," he said with impatience. "Read the story."

Fernie skimmed it. Penny had been driving the family car late at night, after a quick trip to the grocery store, when it suddenly sped up and went off a curve into a ravine. The police believed that she'd accidentally pressed the accelerator when she'd really wanted to press the brake. It was the kind of thing that could have happened to any innocent driver who wasn't paying enough attention to what she was doing.

The story also reported that Penny's husband, Hans, after having been notified at home of her death, collapsed in shock and had been taken to a local hospital for observation. Howard Philip October, a "family friend" who had been staying with the couple, gave a statement instead, telling the newspaper, "Penny was an extraordinarily good person with a kind heart and a gentle soul. The worst part of this tragedy is that she would have been a terrific mother."

There was that phrase again. *Would have been.*

But that wasn't even the startling part. Fernie read the sentence three times to make sure she'd read it correctly, and then looked up at Gustav, feeling dazed. "She didn't die after you were born. She died *before*."

"I told you," Gustav said with a petulance she had never seen in him. "She wasn't my mother. She *would have been* my mother. She died three months too soon to be my mother."

"B-but . . . how is that even possible? You're standing right there, in front of me, and—"

"My father was in the hospital for three days," Gustav said without answering her question. "He returned to the Gloom house, hating the place for the first time in his life, because it was even bigger and emptier without her, and because there were reminders of her, and of the child who would now never be born, everywhere he looked. He was heartbroken and saw no reason to go on living in the house inside the house. He told his good friend Howard Philip October that he'd spend a couple of days gathering up his things, and hers, and then leave town forever.

"From what I've been told, Howard Philip October just smiled sadly, put a hand on my father's shoulder, and told him that he understood. He said, 'Stay as long as you like.'"

Anger burned in Gustav's black eyes. "October said it like it was his house, not my father's, and it was up to him to give permission. My father didn't even notice. He barely had enough energy to think. The packing that should have taken a day stretched to three, and then to four . . . before everything changed."

Fernie didn't want to ask Gustav the next question. "What happened?"

"Somebody who witnessed her death told

my father what had really happened to Penny. She told him that Penny had been in full control of the car and paying full attention to everything she was doing when the gas pedal suddenly pressed itself to the floor, the steering wheel ripped itself out of her hands, and the car headed for that ravine on its own. A truck passed by in the other lane, with its headlights on high, and lit up the inside of Penny's car for a second, long enough for her to see that the car all around her was filled with shadows, fighting her for control of the car. Penny recognized one of them as October's. She was still begging October's shadow for the life of her baby when the car went over the edge."

Gustav fell silent and lowered his head, just as if he were remembering that day himself, even though he hadn't been there and could only report what he'd been told.

Fernie didn't understand who could have told Gustav the story in that much detail, and was about to ask. But then a more terrible thought occurred to her. She realized that the future Gustav actually *had* been there, inside Penny, and that killing her had also been, by definition, an attempt to kill him.

Her mouth was so dry that her voice broke even as she asked the next question. "What did your father do when he found out?"

"What any husband in that situation would do," Gustav said. "He went off to find and confront the man who had pretended to be his friend."

He took the album from her, closed it with an audible *snap*, and tossed it back onto the bed.

He said, "I wish I could tell you what happened next. I don't know what happened between October and my father. I don't know how October wound up becoming a shadow eater. I only know that after that day, neither my father nor Howard Philip October was ever seen again."

Fernie now understood why the walls of the house inside the house reeked of sadness. She could picture Gustav's father, lying in his crazy bed, thinking of everything he had lost and how empty his life would now be, with nothing to show for it but a family photo album that had accumulated all the happy pictures it ever would. She couldn't even imagine what must have gone through his mind when the witness, whoever she was, reported October's involvement . . . or how often Gustav himself must have visited this place, looked through those same pictures, and missed people he had never been given a chance to know.

The air suddenly grew much, much colder, and a voice outside cried, "Girl! October has found you!"

Gustav raced past her, down the hallway, and into the nursery. Fernie followed close behind and saw the same view he saw out the window: the terrible form of the shadow eater, standing in the center of the fake lawn, sniffing the air for signs of them.

"Come out now, girl! You do not want to make me come after you!"

Terrified, Fernie asked Gustav, "What are you going to do?"

"What do you think I'm going to do? I'm going to march right up to October and ask him some tough questions."

Fernie could only protest: "But you can't just walk up to him, not with the things he can do. You need a plan."

"Do you have one?" Gustav demanded.

"No."

"Do you know where we can go about finding one?"

"No."

"Do you know where Great-Aunt Mellifluous and the others are hiding so we can ask *them* if they have any ideas?"

"No."

"Can you think of anybody else, anywhere, who can tell us anything about what this Nightmare Vault is and why October wants it?"

She would have preferred giving any other answer in the world, but found herself forced to a frightened, unwilling, "No."

"Then," Gustav said, with inescapable logic, "he's the only one left. We'll talk to him, all right. We just won't talk to him *here*."

He walked past a still-sputtering Fernie, left the bedroom, and marched down the stairs.

She whirled around and ran down the stairs after him, just in time to look over the side and see him heading down the central hallway for the kitchen at the rear of the house.

The kitchen turned out to be the only room in the house that showed its long years of abandonment. There was still no dust, nor any mess, but the cabinets lining the walls had all had their doors removed and been emptied of any supplies they might have once housed. The sink was pristine, and the tiled floor showed indentations where heavy appliances might have stood. The only obvious cutlery, a set of cutting knives, sat in a slot holder in the middle of the central island. The only other item left over from its days as a working kitchen was a roll of aluminum foil.

A doorway off to the right led to another chamber that might have been a laundry room, but from where Fernie stood looked as empty as everything else. It was as if the strange forces inside the Gloom house had reached inside the smaller house inside the house and claimed all the modern things as soon as Hans and Penny Gloom were gone.

Outside, October cried, "This is your last warning! Bring me to the Nightmare Vault!"

Gustav stood at the open screen door to the backyard, waiting for her. He whispered, "I'll get you back outside first, if you want. There's no reason we both have to talk to him."

It was a tempting offer. Fernie couldn't help worrying about Pearlie and their dad and even Harrington, and would have liked nothing more than to run back outside and give them all reassuring hugs. But she had been through so much with Gustav that the thought of his trying to keep her away from the same dangers he had to face infuriated her. "The man walked into my house and ate my shadow. Don't you think *I* might have a few things to say?"

Gustav seemed a little stunned and humbled by the reminder. "I'm sorry, Fernie. I almost forgot all about what he did to you. You're right. That was pretty rude of him, too."

"Not just pretty rude," Fernie said. "*Cosmically* rude."

Gustav seemed to appreciate that. "He is a big jerk, isn't he?"

"And he's smelly," Fernie added.

Gustav cocked his head a little. "I know I never got all that close, but I didn't notice the smelly part. Is he really?"

Fernie thought back to her first meeting with the man. "No. It's just something else to say as long as we're calling him names. He wasn't smelly. We can erase the smelly."

"That's not necessary. I'm perfectly okay with calling him smelly. I was just checking." Gustav held the door open for her and offered her a little bow. "After you."

CHAPTER TEN
THE SUN IN THE SKY
OVER THE HOUSE INSIDE THE HOUSE

The backyard of the house inside the house was another lawn made out of lush green carpet, surrounded by walls painted the same color as the sky. The light of the "sun" over the front yard was not as direct here, so the sky was painted darker and bore a number of pinprick lights, like the first stars becoming visible in the early light of a warm country evening. An empty hammock, which looked as comforting as all hammocks do, dangled between two upright poles, inviting Fernie or anybody else who passed by for a nice nap. Fernie almost wanted to, but she'd learned on the first trip inside the Gloom house that some places that looked inviting were just traps, promising terrible fates to anybody who heeded their calls.

The thought made her shiver, which wasn't hard to do because the air was so unnaturally cold. That made her think of the "sun," whose glow she could still make out over the edge of the little house's roof. What she could see really did look like a glowing ball of fire, one that from this angle seemed to be setting on the other side of the house. Some of the shadow eater's tendrils rose toward it, like smoke. Others curled around the house inside the house, like blind snakes searching a burrow for mice to eat.

Despite the imminent danger, Fernie had to ask. "Gustav? Before we go, what is that thing?"

Gustav followed her gaze and said, "That? It's our sun."

"No, I mean really."

"So do I," Gustav said.

"Gustav—" she began.

"In a minute." He turned his attention to the wall marking the end of the little house's backyard, where a single lonely doorknob interrupted the expansive mural of faraway countryside. It was an odd place for a doorknob, in that there were no seams around it marking the presence of an actual door. But he turned it anyway, and when he did, the entire rear wall swung backward. There was no need to open it more than a crack. The narrow opening was as shrouded in darkness as the house inside the house was bathed in sunlight, but Gustav stepped over this threshold without fear, and Fernie followed close behind.

Once they were past it, Gustav closed the door behind him and lit a candle he must have been carrying with him, creating a cozy circle of light that revealed the space around them to be a narrow hallway, leading into the darkness to both his left and right.

"Come on," he said, breaking into a jog.

Fernie hustled along behind him. "Won't he chase us?"

"From what Great-Aunt Mellifluous warned me, he's not very talented at tracking anybody who keeps moving. He's a terror when it comes to finding people who've settled down in a hiding place, because anyone staying in one place heats the air in a way he can sense from a distance, but he loses all track of anyone who keeps going. Don't you already feel better?"

Now that Gustav mentioned it, the terrible chill around them seemed to be fading. "But we can't keep going forever!"

"No. We can't. But we can keep going long enough to choose the place where he catches up. Come on."

The narrow passageway stretched out before them for what seemed like miles. After a few minutes, they slowed down a little, and Fernie prodded, "The sun?"

"Oh, that. It's not actually the sun you're used to looking at. Not the whole thing, anyway. It's just a little piece of it, brought down to Earth and cooled just enough so that we can keep it around without burning up."

One of the stranger things about visiting the Gloom house more than once is that you could hear something like that and believe it immediately. This was not the same thing as not having any problems with it. "What are you doing with a piece of the *sun* hanging over your head in your *house*?"

"All shadow houses contain a ball of concentrated sunlight. They need one around, because while shadows prefer darkness, they also can't exist without light. This is ours. My grandfather built the house inside the house here, just under it, because he didn't want to look out his front window and see a dark room all the time."

This was all worse than no explanation at all, because it failed to account for just who had gone out and collected a little piece of the sun, and how Gustav himself could walk around underneath it when she'd seen him start to vaporize like a movie vampire the second he was exposed to the direct rays of the real sun in the real sky.

You could collect a lot of question marks when having a simple conversation in the Gloom house. It was safer, sometimes, to go with the first answers that were given, and say what Fernie said now: "Okay."

They reached the end of the narrow passage they traveled, made a left turn, and kept going.

A few minutes later, they reached an intersection and turned right.

Fearing that Gustav had led her into another situation like the endless train of closets, Fernie finally exploded, "But where does this lead?"

"Everywhere," he said.

"Gustav!"

"No, I'm serious. You can get anywhere in the house from these passages."

"What is that? More shadow tricks?"

"No. They're actually a real-world thing, left over from the days when the Gloom house was still a normal house, if you really can use that word to describe a big mansion with a small army of maids and butlers on staff. Back then, servants weren't supposed to be seen unless they were needed, so they traveled from one part of the house to another through hallways that ran behind all the other rooms, and did all their cleaning and so on while out of sight. The trick was to avoid being seen. I've been taught that in some houses like this, a maid could actually get fired if the boss happened to walk in and catch her dusting."

Fernie said, "Couldn't she also get fired if he walked in and found her *not* dusting?"

"I suppose," he supposed. "The trick for the servants was always to pretend that they weren't there and that the mess was always picked up and the dust always wiped away and the windows always cleared of smudges all by themselves, without a couple dozen busy people running around hidden hallways and popping into rooms doing all the work." He thought about it for a moment, and said, "I guess that made it a shadow house of a different kind, then."

Fernie and Gustav turned left at a four-way intersection and hurried down a passage so narrow that they had to rush along single file,

Gustav's candle illuminating no more than the few steps ahead and the few steps back.

A little while later, they arrived at another four-way intersection, and Gustav turned right, into a corridor even narrower than the one before it; so narrow, in fact, that Fernie could have named a number of people, Mrs. Everwiner, for example, who would have been too fat to pass.

Another left turn and the passage narrowed yet again, giving Fernie the impression of walls closing in, eager to crush her. They reached a thin set of stairs, climbed it, made their way down another long and narrow hallway, and reached another stairwell, which they climbed as well.

Five flights of stairs later, Fernie found herself getting winded. "How high are we climbing?"

Gustav said, "High enough to stay out of his reach long enough to ask what needs to be asked. The grand parlor goes up high enough that he might find answering our questions easier than chasing us."

"Doesn't that all depend on his being on the ground floor of the parlor?"

"It does," Gustav allowed, "but that's more or less the first place I would go, if I were him and needed to catch our scent again. If not, I think we can still attract his attention."

Gustav and Fernie climbed more flights, and further conversation lagged as they forced themselves as far as they could go. On the way, Fernie couldn't help but notice how quiet the house seemed. On her previous visit, the place had been anything but silent; even in the most isolated places, there had always been distant whispers, cries, breathing, the sounds a living house makes when people, or at least creatures, move around inside. But now all the shadows were in hiding, and the walls around them seemed as quiet as a tomb. Her own ragged breath reflected the exhaustion of a girl who might have been able to run up ten flights of stairs without breathing hard, but was being pushed to her limits by the time she had climbed twenty.

If this had been less important, she might have asked Gustav for a break.

She lost count of how far they had climbed, though it was certainly much higher than the house seen from the outside should have been able to accommodate.

Then he sat down at the top of one flight that looked the same as any other flight and wiped a thin sheen of sweat from his forehead. He was tired, but not nearly as out of breath as Fernie was. "Okay," he said. "This is the floor with the gong. We should rest up a bit before we strike it, because we might have to run away in a hurry if things go wrong."

Fernie sat down gratefully. "Gong?"

"Yes," Gustav said. "It's a giant round bell, about this big." He extended his arms as far as they would go.

"I know . . . what a . . . gong is. But what's one . . . doing all the way up here?" she panted.

"I brought it up from the basement," Gustav explained.

"You . . . carried . . . a gong . . . up all these stairs?"

"I don't want to pretend I'm stronger than I am," he said. "It took me four days. I had help, and even then I had to drag it a little bit farther every day."

"Why . . . would you . . . spend four days . . . lugging a big heavy . . . gong . . . through all those . . . narrow hallways . . . and up more than twenty . . . flights of stairs?"

"So I could ring it," he said as if that were the most obvious question in the world.

She was mad at herself for falling into the same trap that she'd promised herself she wouldn't fall into again of asking questions.

But this time, he surprised her by offering the explanation. "Look, it's very simple. Remember that time from your last visit when we fell down the garbage chute into a big pile of shadow-stuff? Remember how far we fell and how soft the landing was?"

Fernie remembered. It had been just like landing in a big pile of feathers.

"Wasn't that fun?" he asked.

Now that she thought about it, it had been. "Yes."

"Well," he said, "there's no place in the house with a greater distance to fall, or with more shadows crowded together on the ground below me, than the balconies high above the grand parlor. I ring the gong because they can hear it and be warned that I'm about to jump. So far, they've always made a big soft pile out of themselves to cushion my landing."

It sounded exactly like the kind of fun thing Fernie would have wanted to try, even if it was also the kind of thing her dad would call an accident waiting to happen. But something bothered her. "Didn't you also tell me that most of the shadows here don't really care whether you live or die?"

"Pretty much all of them," he agreed. "There are only a few exceptions, like Great-Aunt Mellifluous, Mr. Notes's shadow, and Fluffy the Dinosaur, who you haven't met yet."

She ignored the reference to Fluffy the Dinosaur.

"And yet you're willing to jump from high balconies, for fun, just because there *might* be enough of them eager to catch you as long as they hear you ring the gong first?"

Gustav blinked at her, as uncomprehending as he might have been if she'd said that there were giraffes in her underwear, or that there were swimming pools filled with yams on the moon. "It's always worked so far."

Being Gustav's friend sometimes meant wanting to slap him on the top of the head.

Fernie might have done just that, but before she could, he saw that she was rested enough, and gestured for her to follow him again. "Come on," he said. "It's time."

They emerged from the maze of narrow servants' passageways onto a chilly abandoned walkway, a skyscraping height over the grand parlor far below. It was far from the highest balcony, as the atrium extended upward as far as Fernie's eyes could see, the nested balconies above them continuing to reach for the sky until they disappeared in a haze. But this was as high as she would have wanted to climb, given that none of the floors this high up seemed to have railings. It was also nastier in other ways, with spiderwebs making tents in the space between walls and floor, and a thin layer of dirt that crunched beneath her shoes every time she took a step.

The gong stood about twenty steps from the entrance to the servants' passageway, as out of place as a bunny on a motorcycle. It was even larger than Gustav had indicated, a head taller than him and about half again as wide as the span of his arms. Fernie was impressed that he'd been able to move it at all, let alone drag it down so many narrow hallways and up so many flights of stairs.

It was an ornate gong, with serpentine golden dragons curled around the frame it hung from and two intertwined fish on the great golden disk itself. Diamonds and rubies and emeralds glittered wherever it might have occurred to its previous owners to put some. Fernie would not have been surprised to find out that it had once stood in the palace of an emperor. It was, after all, the kind of thing an emperor would have, probably so some slave could ring it every time the boss said something particularly decisive.

Either way, she could tell that it was an ancient treasure, probably worth many times more than everything her family owned put together. Gustav had dragged it up out of the basement so he could play with it.

The beater was a padded, weighted tool the size of a sledgehammer, hanging from two prongs on the side of the arch-shaped frame. The striking end looked heavy enough to shatter brick walls. Fernie thought that she would have had more than enough trouble carrying *that* up so many flights of stairs, without also worrying about the gong.

Gustav stood at the edge of the balcony and looked down, leaning out a little just to be sure. He teetered as if about to fall, then rocked back on his heels. "He's not down there. Either he's gone back outside or he's still exploring, somewhere."

Fernie peered over the edge as well and saw the tiled floor of the grand parlor, a tiny checkerboard studded with toy furniture many stories below. From here, the two dozen stairways of different types that rose from that level to various levels higher up looked like thin lines, crisscrossing that distant space as if to strike out the whole place, marking the room like a mistake on a test paper. Another danger of Gustav's reckless jumping hobby occurred to her: A leap meant not just hoping the shadows saw fit to cushion his landing, but also first aiming carefully enough to make sure that he didn't smash himself against some set of stairs before the shadows even had a chance. The mental image this gave her was not pretty. She shuddered and took a hasty step away from the edge.

Gustav lifted the gong beater off its hooks and cradled it in both arms before getting a firm grip on the handle and letting the striker hit the floor with an audible *thunk*. "Better stand back," he said. "And get ready. If he answers, we might have to run in a hurry."

Fernie hesitated. After everything she'd seen, she wasn't sure she was ready to face the shadow eater again. But then, she didn't think she ever would be as ready as she would have liked to be. That, she reflected, was the major challenge of facing monsters. Sometimes you had to give up on being "ready," and just get on with it. She took a deep breath and said, "Okay."

Gustav nodded. "On three."

CHAPTER ELEVEN
A NICE LEISURELY CHAT
WITH HOWARD PHILIP OCTOBER

Fernie retreated against the wall to give Gustav enough room for his most powerful swing. Just as he strained to lift the beater over his shoulder, she obeyed a sudden impulse and stuck her fingers in her ears.

It was not the loveliest swing in the history of the world. The slaves responsible for beating that gong, in whatever emperor's palace it had come from, might have laughed at Gustav's weakness, even if he was just a kid. But gravity took over on the downswing, and the beater hit the gong dead center, hard enough to leave Fernie happy to have protected her ears. The ring was not just loud but deafening, with a keening follow-up vibration that she could feel in her teeth.

If anything, the bong seemed to get louder, not quieter, as the next seconds went on. The note echoed throughout the empty space of the atrium, hitting the walls and bouncing against other walls and making the single gong strike sound like a dozen, all almost as loud as the first. The sound must have been as impossible to ignore on the ground floor as it was all the way up on the balcony, and it only grew more insistent as Gustav drew back the beater and struck the gong a second time, and a third.

"Hey!" Gustav yelled. The note was still reverberating. *"Howard Philip October! Where are you? I'm caaaallling you! Come out, come out, wherever you are!"*

He leaned over the edge to look down.

"Come on, Howard Philip October! Stop hiding! You want the Nightmare Vault, I'm the one to talk to! Show your face now and I won't even say anything about it being so ugly! Come on, Howard Philip October! I'm talking to you!"

His own voice echoed, too, until the atrium before them rang with multiple mocking repetitions of *Howard Philip October*, bouncing off the balconies like a thousand Ping-Pong balls looking for a place to land.

After a moment, he seemed to see something. "There he is." And he shouted again: *"Up here, smelly! That's right! I'm talking to you!"*

Fernie felt a chill as the air around them grew perceptibly colder. She ventured toward the edge to look down and see a great swirling mass of darkness, like a bowl of ebony spaghetti, writhing on the lower floors. A man-shaped white speck stood in the center of that darkness and seemed to be slowly rising toward the level where Gustav and Fernie stood.

Her heart thumped. "How did you know he'd be able to fly?"

"That's not so much flying as climbing," Gustav said.

"But how did you know?"

"I didn't. I figured. As long as that shadow-stuff inside him is able to reach out and grab things, it should be able to climb."

"How does *that* help?" Fernie wanted to know.

"It gives us the few minutes it'll take him to get here. We'll be able to have a nice leisurely talk with him without worrying about his grabbing us right away."

Fernie steeled herself for another glance over the side. The swirling mass of blackness had now swallowed most of the lower crisscrossing stairways. The man-shaped thing at its center was now easier to make out as the same one who had chased Fernie and her sister from their home. At the rate he was climbing, he was going to be upon Fernie and Gustav in less than a minute.

"Are we going to have time?" she worried.

"I think we'll make time," Gustav said.

She risked another look down. The leading tendrils were now only five stories or so below them. "Now?"

"I want to look him in the face," Gustav said.

Fernie gave the rising figure another look. The space where his face should have been was the big black O of his open mouth, larger than any face would have been.

Gustav glanced down and guessed what she was thinking. "Good point. That is disgusting." He yelled again: *"All right, Howard Philip October! That's close enough! Come any closer and you'll never get your Nightmare Vault!"*

To Fernie's surprise, the figure in the yellowing white uniform stopped rising, only four stories below them. His mouth closed most of the way, his lumpy features drawing back over the yawning black emptiness of his mouth like an ill-fitting hood. His unhappy eyes searched for the source of the threat, found Gustav, and regarded him without any obvious understanding or recognition. But his body turned and shifted closer to their side of the atrium so he could stare up at Fernie and the boy with her.

He was as slow at forming sentences as he had been inside Fernie's home, and when he spoke, through a mouth still sprouting dozens of long black tendrils, it was unclear whether he was answering Gustav or speaking to himself and not caring whether Gustav heard. He was close enough now to speak in a conversational tone of voice. "You're the girl who ran," he noted in his lifeless voice. "The one I'll have to punish for making me give chase. The boy, I don't know. Who are you, boy?"

While staying the same size and remaining the same boy, Gustav seemed to swell, and darken, and become something far more terrible than the boy Fernie knew, who had never tasted fried chicken and was capable of wondering whether pizza was some kind of bird.

"Who am I?" he roared, in tones so fearsome Fernie wondered why he'd ever bothered to use a gong. "You come into *my* house, scare *my* friends, chase away *my* family, and dare to ask who *I* am? You could not possibly be so stupid!

My name's Gustav Gloom. Grandson of Lemuel Gloom, son of Hans, almost the son of Penelope, protector of this house and of my friends. If you're looking for anything inside these walls, you need to negotiate with ME."

Fernie was sincerely impressed. "Wow."

Even October seemed a little intimidated. He retreated a few feet, as if considering that information. Then he looked up again, his lumpy cheeks bulging and twisting from the shapes churning beneath them. "Very well, boy. I will deal with you. Where's the Nightmare Vault?"

"Not so fast, smelly," said Gustav, speaking in a conversational tone of voice now that the proper respect had been offered. "I've spent my whole life in this place, have explored it more than you could in a thousand years, and still don't even know what you're talking about. I'm not going to help you look without trading some questions for answers, starting with just what this Nightmare Vault looks like."

October took several seconds to think on this, his uniformed body bobbing in the air just below the spot where Gustav stood. When he spoke, his voice sounded like a cry at the bottom of a deep well. "Is this a trick?"

"I can't tell you where to find something if I

don't know what it looks like."

"It will be in a wooden cabinet. Ten feet tall, four feet wide, three feet deep, standing on four clawed legs. There are two big doors in front, opening in the middle. There are two handles in the center, held shut with heavy chains."

Gustav shrugged his shoulders so gently that only Fernie could see it. He hadn't ever seen any furniture in the house that fit October's quick description.

"Maybe I know what you're talking about and maybe I don't. Maybe I need some persuading that it's something you should be allowed to have. What's in it?"

"Nightmares," October said.

"You're pretty nightmarish already. Just look at you. You're so powerful that people and shadows both run away from you. What power will the Nightmare Vault give you that you don't already have?"

October's forehead swelled, then shrank, as if reflecting the fury of the thoughts within. "The cabinet is not for the October who stands before you. It is for his master."

"But if you don't know where it is, how do you know it exists?"

"When October was still human, he read Lemuel Gloom's book. There's a chapter on the Nightmare Vault. October offered Lemuel Gloom millions for it. Lemuel Gloom said no man should have it. He said that October would never have it."

This struck Fernie as a pretty sound business decision on Lemuel Gloom's part.

October droned on. "Later on, October moved into the Gloom house. He found many powerful things. He made many shadow allies. He still could not find the Nightmare Vault. He was afraid when Hans and Penny Gloom moved back in. He could not afford to be stopped before he found what he wanted. But he made a mistake. He thought Hans would also be in the car. But only Penny was in the car. Only Penny died when the car went over the edge."

Gustav's profile, which looked serious at the best of times, now looked downright grim, and his pale skin had turned a light pink that might have been as close as it could ever get to being scarlet with fury.

October had started to rise again and was now less than ten feet below the balcony where they stood. He was so close that it was possible to see into the darkness inside the mouth, see the storm clouds that churned inside him, as fresh tendrils spilled from his lips. Fernie noticed what she hadn't before: a couple of the leading tendrils curling over the edge of the balcony, not making much of a show out of their advance, but definitely approaching Gustav like sly dogs trying to pretend they weren't really interested in that piece of turkey carelessly left on the kitchen counter.

She said, "Gustav . . ."

He gestured her silent with a wave of his hand and addressed October again. "One last question. What happened between you and my father after he found out what you had done?"

The tendrils gripping the edge of the balcony where Gustav and Fernie stood suddenly retreated, as if burned by the surface of a hot stove.

October's mouth formed an expression that was neither smile nor grimace, snarl nor leer, but something that might have been all of them, possible only on a mouth that could stretch farther than any human mouth ever had. It was like a shark's grin, with no joy or friendliness or humor behind it: just an open mouth, unconnected to anything that he might have been thinking or feeling.

He said, "Your father went after October. He hunted October through the house for thirteen days and thirteen nights. He fought monsters to get to October. He went without rest to get to October. He never let up. He chased October through all the terrible rooms of this house, all the way to the pit leading to the Dark Country."

"And then?" Gustav demanded.

"They fell in together, clutching each other as only deadly enemies can, still fighting all the way down."

Fernie heard a sudden loud *crunch* at her feet. She looked down and saw something that terrified her: a dark, shadowy tendril, exploring the floor around the hole it had punched through the underside of the balcony. It almost found her left shoe before she stepped away, but even as she did there was another *crunch* and yet another dark tendril broke through, whipping through the hole it had made like a black snake.

More crunches followed, dozens of them in every direction, each of them followed by another tendril of the shadows at October's command. In seconds there was a forest of them, grasping the air for the girl they knew to be standing somewhere on the floor they had broken through.

October bellowed: *"Now give me the Nightmare Vault!"*

Fernie kicked at one of the tendrils, and it reared back, as if both enraged to have been attacked and delighted to have found her. It grabbed for her, faster than she'd seen any of them move before.

Without thinking, she leaped over its lunge and landed on her feet right behind Gustav, who was also surrounded by them but didn't seem to care enough about that to take his grim eyes off the distorted, grinning face of Howard Philip October.

Gustav didn't raise his voice. "Before I'm done, you're going to wish you had stayed where my father sent you."

Then he put his back against the gong's massive frame and pushed.

It was too heavy to fall immediately, but Fernie saw what he was doing and lent her own shoulder to the effort. At first it seemed like the gong wasn't going to move at all, and Fernie groaned from the strain as the black tendrils emerging from the floor groped for her, but then the gong started to tip toward the edge.

The two kids braced their shoes against the floor and their backs against the frame and strained with all their might, until the slight tilt became a greater one and the gong started to fall.

Fernie had put so much of her weight into it that she took an unwilling step or two after it went and started to go over the edge herself. For one terrible moment, she saw nothing below her but yawning open space, the tumbling gong, and the terrible form of the man who had been Howard Philip October.

She spun her arms and managed to stay upright long enough to see October's face at the moment when he saw that he would not be able to avoid the gong. It was the same expression anybody would have when looking up and seeing a heavy falling object. Inhuman as October was, he did not seem to look forward to the impact.

The sound the gong made as it landed flat against his face was far louder than the tones Gustav had managed to make with the beater, but then the gong landed on October much harder than the head of the beater had landed on it. Even so, October almost managed to drown out that resounding note with his own cry of pain and rage. The impact drove him down almost three full stories, and might have sent him plummeting all the way to the parlor floor, but the shadow tendrils managed to recover, grab hold of another balcony, and start pulling him back up. The gong flipped away and continued to fall, its work done. There was now a sizable dent in the center of the bell.

This all happened in about a second or so, in the time Fernie spent spinning her arms at the edge of the balcony, trying not to fall. Now she screamed as she tipped forward over the edge farther than any amount of frantic arm-waving could have possibly corrected.

October's face, which had been misshapen before, now looked like one giant bruise. More black tendrils spilled from his mouth and reached up for her.

Then a small but strong hand grabbed the back of her shirt and with a single tug pulled her back from the edge.

Gustav looked paler than she'd ever seen him. "Don't ever scare me like that."

Fernie felt pretty pale herself. "I'll try not to."

The crunching sounds resumed. More black tendrils punched holes in the balcony floor. As the two friends ran together toward the entrance to the servants' corridor, the tendrils grew so furious at their failure to catch the children that they began tearing the balcony to splinters. One giant section was ripped away just as Gustav and Fernie were about to run across it. There was no time to stop, so they leaped together, landing in a heap on the other side, which also started to collapse beneath them.

Far below them, the gong rang as it smashed into the floor of the grand parlor.

Gustav and Fernie scrambled to their feet and ran the rest of the way to the servants' passage, tossing the narrow door open and barreling down the stairs, once again ahead of the tendrils pursuing them. Gustav no longer had a lit candle, so for long minutes they fled through nearly total darkness, Fernie unable to do anything but follow the dimly glimpsed figure up ahead.

From time to time he shouted a warning at her: "Left turn!" or "Stairs!" She hit a wall face-first, bounced off, almost headed the wrong way, and was guided back by another Gustav yell: "No, here!"

They didn't stop running until Gustav pulled Fernie into a narrow space beneath a narrow flight of stairs. After that, they sat side by side, panting, both struggling to get their breathing under control so their gasps wouldn't drown out any sounds of walls being torn down in October's determination to catch them.

After a long time, their breath quieted.

Fernie glanced at the boy beside her and ached to see past the darkness. After all, this hadn't been a good night for him. He'd been abandoned by his adoptive family. He had been reminded of his tragic past. He had confronted and fought his first battle with the evil man who'd killed the woman who *would have been* his mother. He'd learned the fate of his father. She couldn't even imagine what he was thinking.

Then he heaved one of the most forlorn sighs she had ever heard and told her.

He said, "I'm really going to miss that gong."

CHAPTER TWELVE
THE MOST FEARED CREATURE IN THE GLOOM HOUSE

They rested for a bit, then got up so Gustav could lead her through more of the servants' passages, following a route that must have made some kind of sense to him, even though Fernie saw it as just a lot of running around heading nowhere in particular.

They had descended several flights of stairs and inched their way through what Fernie estimated to be several miles of corridor when she finally lost patience and exclaimed, "Do we have a plan yet?"

Gustav said, "No."

"Do we have a plan for *coming up with* a plan?"

"No."

"Do you even know where we're going?"

"Sure I do."

"Where?"

He pointed in the direction they happened to be walking. "This way."

"Does *this way* lead anywhere that might be helpful, or is it just the way we happen to be going?"

He asked, "Does your dad ever get irritated with you on long trips?"

"No," she retorted, "but we've never been on any when we were being chased by shadow eaters."

A few minutes later they stopped at a spot that looked the same as every other, and Gustav pressed the palms of his hands against the wall. It swung open at his touch and revealed a solemn, empty chamber that Fernie had never seen before. It was the kind of long, narrow room that would have qualified as a hallway if the sides had been squeezed together a little bit. There was no furniture, but the walls were lined with framed portraits.

The men wore monocles, top hats, muttonchops, and the annoyed frowns of people who had just been interrupted while making important decisions. The women wore towering hairstyles that must have taken them all day to arrange and might have presented a problem with any nearby low-hanging ceiling fans. They all looked like famous people trying to hold the same fixed expressions on their faces for however long it took artists to paint them. The room was lit by candles burning in glass fixtures mounted on the wall between each painting.

"This is the Gallery of the Almost Famous," Gustav said. "They're all people who could have done important things but never got around to it." He pointed at one fellow with a bald head and a mustache so broad that people standing directly behind him must have been able to see both tips sticking out the sides. "Like this one here: According to the plaque, his name was Colonel Montgomery J. Summerbottom, and he was going to mount an expedition to the South Pole, but decided not to go at the last minute because he'd just found out for the first time that it might be cold."

"Gustav, how does this *help* us?"

"The painting? Not at all. But we can use this." He unscrewed the glass globe between the painting of Colonel Summerbottom and the painting next to it of a very proper woman who looked like she wanted to sneeze.

He handed the globe to Fernie.

She stared at the globe, which was sooty and warm from the fire it had contained. "What am I supposed to do with this?"

"I think we'll need it," Gustav said.

"So you were lying. You do have a plan."

"I never lie," Gustav said. "I don't have a plan, or even a plan for *coming up with* a plan. What I do have is an *idea*."

"What's the difference?"

"An *idea* comes first, and is what you have when you know something that might work, but still need to figure out how to go about it. A *plan* is what you have when you know what you're going to do and how you're going to do it. I have the *idea*, but no *plan* yet."

Fernie thought that over and decided that in Gustav-land, it made a certain amount of sense. "All right," she said. "So you may not have any plan for coming up with a plan, but does your *idea* give you any *ideas* about how to come up with a plan?"

"Of course," Gustav said. "I'm going to go ask an old acquaintance of mine for advice."

"I thought you said that there was nobody to ask but October."

"That wasn't quite true. I do know someone else who should still be around, but he's not exactly a friend and not easy to have a useful conversation with."

Fernie was left wondering what kind of old acquaintance could possibly be so unpleasant that Gustav would have found him harder to talk to than the shadow eater.

Gustav went to the light fixture on the other side of Summerbottom's portrait, unscrewed its globe as well, and took that one for himself. "I am pretty sure about one thing: That wasn't the real Howard Philip October."

"But you said—"

He started for the set of double doors at the far side of the room, forcing Fernie to hurry in order to catch up with him. "I never said it was him. I showed you a picture of October and asked you if it was the same man you saw. You said it was. That's not the same thing as *my* saying it was, and now that I've met him and talked to him I don't think it was."

She rushed along beside him, not getting it at all. "Why not?"

"He didn't *sound* like Howard Philip October."

"How would you know, if he disappeared before you were born?"

"I told you, he wrote books. I've read them all just in case he ever tried to come back, and even listened to some recordings my grandfather had of his voice. He was the kind of person who doesn't really know what he's talking about but thinks he can fool you into thinking he does by using long windy sentences and words that sound important but that he doesn't really understand."

"Like what?"

"Well, like for instance, *squamous*."

"You're just making that up."

"No. It means 'covered in little scales.' In his books, he kept using it to describe people he had met. If you listened to him, he couldn't travel fifteen feet in any direction without finding people who looked squamous. Why, I read one of his books where he took a trip to some spooky little village somewhere and, if you believe him, every single person he met there was squamous."

"If the village really was that spooky, maybe they were."

"Maybe. Or maybe he was just counting on nobody who read his books owning a dictionary. The point is that the real Howard Philip October used a lot of fancy words, even if he didn't always use them the right way. That thing we just met could barely come up with a *the*."

"Maybe becoming whatever he is now hurt his mind."

"Could be," Gustav said. "But I think the real October is still alive somewhere, and that this one is just a bad copy, one that looks like October and has some of his memories, but still isn't really him."

"Is he October's shadow?"

"No. He's filled with shadows, but his skin, the part that gets all lumpy because of the shadows moving around inside him, is human. It might even be grown from October's own skin, since it looks so much like him, but I don't think there's anything else inside that thing but the shadows he's eaten."

"How does that help?" she wanted to know.

"I don't know," he said honestly. "But it might be something we need to keep in mind."

They reached the set of double doors at the end of the Gallery of the Almost Famous. Gustav propped his glass globe under one arm in order to handle the doorknob with the other, hesitated, and told Fernie, "I should warn you. When we open the door, we might have to run very fast."

"Gee," Fernie said. "That would be a nice change."

"I'm serious. We're about to head into a part of the house where the shadows aren't very civilized. Most of them aren't evil so much as mean and unpleasant. They're not fit for polite company, and are so disliked by most of the others that they band together here, where nobody talks to them or has anything to do with them."

"Is it a jail?" she asked.

"No. There's a jail here, and it happens to be where we're going . . . but everything around it is like . . . a bad neighborhood. It's possible they were never warned about the shadow eater, and might not have hidden wherever the rest went. They'll give us trouble if we try to pass."

"Then why do we have to go this way?"

"Because," Gustav said, "it's the only way I know of to get to the jail. The person I want to talk to is a prisoner there. Getting to him might be dangerous, and talking to him will be more dangerous still, but we have no other choice, not with October still loose and searching for us."

"Okay," Fernie said. "I'm ready."

Gustav took a deep breath, steeled himself, and pushed open the door.

Fernie was used to seeing dim and dingy places in the Gloom house, but the new corridor on the other side was dimmer and dingier than most: the kind of place not inhabited by mere shadows, but by shadows that couldn't be bothered to keep up appearances. The walls were dirty, as if somebody with mud on his hands had recently passed through and attempted to paint. The air smelled gray with soot, and the carpet runner emitted little puffs of dust with every step Gustav and Fernie took.

They walked quickly, but even so the shadows started to gather around them, circling around to get good looks from all sides. They were not the kind of shadows Fernie had met and come to know, either the good ones like Great-Aunt Mellifluous or the bad ones like the Beast; these were taller, scrawnier, more distorted, almost as if somebody had grabbed them on both ends and stretched them out of shape.

One said, "Boy."

Another said, "I thought we told you to stay out of this part of the house, boy."

Another said, "A halfsie boy could get lost in a place like this and never find his way out."

One of the threatening shadows plucked at Fernie's shirt. It was a nasty pinch that didn't feel anything like the hand of any other shadow whose touch Fernie had known; it felt colder, stickier, as if it had been dipped in gravy and then dried.

"Look, everybody, the girl doesn't have a shadow!"

"Neither does the boy," another shadow pointed out.

"Yes, but we know what the boy is. We've seen him without his shadow before, and know that it always comes back to him. What's the girl's excuse?"

"Maybe she fired it," one theorized.

"Flesh-and-blood people can't fire their shadows," another protested.

"They can if the economy's bad enough," one pointed out.

"We ought to teach her a lesson," another declared.

The shadows looming around Fernie, scandalized by the presence of a flesh-and-blood girl who didn't have a shadow of her own, drew even closer, their cold fingers tugging at her hair to confirm that she was real.

"Walk faster," Gustav murmured.

Fernie did just that, but the shadows continued to gather around her, examining her from head to toe and appearing to block the way ahead.

One piped up with considerable excitement. "Don't hurt her! She's a genuine rarity! We should take her to the zoo, put her in a cage, and charge other shadows to see her!"

The others around him chorused their approval of this excellent idea. "We'll teach her how to do tricks! We'll put on four shows a day!"

More shadows drew close. There seemed to be hundreds of them, all hungry, all cruel, and all frayed at the edges, like ripped cloth. They plucked at Fernie's hair and her clothes, as if greedy for her warmth. Passing through them was like walking through an unseen spiderweb in a dark, cramped place.

Fernie whispered to Gustav, "Do they actually have a zoo where they keep people?"

Gustav whispered back, "They tried to start one with me once. They gave me a tire on a swing, so it wasn't so bad, especially since I got away after a week."

"Wonderful," she muttered.

"I told you we might have to run."

Running seemed pointless now; the corridor in front of them was growing as crowded with disreputable shadows as the corridor behind them. Some were solid enough to have faces, and they were always the stupid, cruel, self-satisfied faces that Fernie associated with schoolyard bullies, taunting weaker kids into begging them to stop. There were so many up ahead that they filled the corridor like fog and made seeing past them impossible. There was no way to know where to run.

The Fernie who had first walked through Gustav Gloom's front door three weeks earlier might have been terrified into running for her life, but this Fernie whirled in place, pointed a pale finger at the nearest shadow's face, and cried, "Would any of you idiots like to know *why* I don't have a shadow?"

They gasped, startled by her question.

One, speaking in a very soft voice, said, "Yes."

She said, "Because I'm a shadow eater and I *ate* mine!"

The disreputable shadows surrounding her all reared back as one at this statement, and for a horrible second or two all seemed about to start laughing at her. But no one shadow seemed prepared to call her a liar until one very slight and meek one ventured, "But a little girl can't be a shadow eater."

"She's bluffing," one of his braver friends declared, though he didn't seem quite sure.

"If I'm bluffing," Fernie said coldly, "then why don't you go check out the Gallery of Awkward Statues, or the Too Much Sitting Room, or the banquet hall, or any of those other places where you used to be able to find all the nice civilized shadows who behaved themselves? Ask yourself why they're all gone."

The uncivilized shadows all gaped at her uneasily, unsure whether to laugh in disbelief or run in terror.

One said, "I haven't heard anything from the rest of the house tonight."

Another protested, "I heard a gong."

An especially irritated one said, "The gong doesn't count. The boy's always beating that gong. Keeping me up all hours of the day and night, when I need my beauty sleep. It's not decent. But that's all I've heard."

Then one of them, speaking in the quavery voice of someone just realizing that he should be afraid, said, "Guys? I ran down to the banquet hall an hour or two ago, hoping for some scraps . . . and she's telling the truth. There was *nobody* there. Why would there be nobody there?"

"Because," Fernie said in the most fearsome voice she could manage, "I ate them all. *And I'm getting hungry again now.*"

The uncivilized shadows decided that fleeing in terror was the better of the two available options, and did just that with a haste that stirred up some of the dust on the floor and sent it trailing after them as if it, too, wanted to flee the unexpectedly frightening little girl.

Surprised that it had worked but gratified to have done something right, she turned back to Gustav, who was giving her the oddest look she'd ever seen him give.

"What?" she asked.

He answered her very softly. "Nothing. That was a very good idea you had. Except . . ."

He was so quiet for so long that she felt the need to prod him. "Except what?"

"You know that they'll go straight to the places you mentioned. And you know that when they do, none of the respectable shadows will be around. This lot will just find empty room after empty room, where all the other shadows used to be. And they'll think you told them the truth. If they manage to avoid October, they'll tell their friends, and so on."

Fernie asked, "And your point?"

He looked away just a fraction of a second too slowly for Fernie to miss the slight twitch at the corners of his lips. He said, "What's the most feared creature in the Gloom house."

"I don't know," she said.

"What," he said.

"Why are you asking me?"

"I wasn't asking you anything, Fernie. I was telling you something. As far as that bunch is concerned, *What* is the most feared creature in the Gloom house. *What*. That's your name. Do you get what I'm saying?"

It took her a second to see what Gustav was getting at. Then she did, and turned red. "Oh."

They walked on in silence through a corridor now blessedly cleared of disreputable shadows, both knowing that it would not be long before the next of the night's many dangers popped up to say hello.

CHAPTER THIRTEEN
FERNIE RECEIVES AN OFFER

For the next few minutes, as they headed deeper into the parts of the house where no respectable shadow would ever go, they weren't bothered. Any shadows they spotted were just terrified, furtive faces peering at them from around corners or through the windowpanes of some of the corridor doors.

The path ahead grew grimmer and dirtier, the air so cold that Fernie could only wonder if somebody had left a window open somewhere. There was so much dust that Fernie had to bite her lip to avoid sneezing.

Then the hairs on the back of Fernie's neck stood straight up, and she sensed something that had been putting her ill at ease for several minutes.

One member of the mob had doubled back to follow them and had now almost caught up with them; even as Fernie whirled to see whom, she cringed, expecting his inevitable cry to his friends, that they should come back, because all the stuff about the little girl being able to eat shadows had been a lie.

Instead, she saw the vague outline of a friendly, skinny figure with bony elbows and knees, and ears that poked out like handles. "Hello, Fernie. Hello, Gustav."

She relaxed. "Hello, Mr. Notes."

Mr. Notes's shadow was one of the few, other than Great-Aunt Mellifluous and Fernie's own shadow, whom Fernie had spoken to. All she really knew about him was that he'd once been the shadow of a mean man also named Mr. Notes, until he decided that following Mr. Notes around was no fun at all.

"I was wondering when you'd catch up with us," Gustav said.

"It took me a while," Mr. Notes's shadow allowed as he fell into a friendly stroll alongside them. "But I had to flee almost all the way to the other end of the house before I could get away from that mob and start making my way back."

Fernie didn't understand. "You were with them?"

"I was the one who told the others that he'd been to the banquet hall looking for scraps. After that wonderfully clever lie you told, it was just the right thing to say to push them the rest of the way into panic."

"Oh." Fernie felt deflated. After how satisfying it had been to scare the disreputable shadows away all by herself, it was disappointing to now find out that she'd had a friend in the mob giving them an extra added nudge.

Gustav spotted her stricken expression. "I'm sorry, Fernie. I thought you knew that it was him. I recognized him right away."

"Well," she said defensively, "I only met him the one time, and even then only for a minute or two. And besides, what was he doing over here with all the disreputable shadows? Why isn't he in hiding with the rest of your family?"

Mr. Notes's shadow seemed a little hurt by that. "Did you really think that Great-Aunt Mellifluous or the other shadows who care about Gustav would leave him *totally* alone during an invasion by a creature as dangerous as the shadow eater? Somebody had to stick around and offer any help we could. Mellifluous asked for volunteers, and I said I'd stay."

Fernie wasn't mollified. "This is the first time we've seen you all night."

"I know, and that's why I said any help we *could*. There was nothing I could do to help you against the shadow eater himself; if I'd gone anywhere near him, I would have been snatched up and eaten and mixed up with all the other shadow-stuff in his belly. I would have become just another one of his tendrils, darting out of his mouth to grab you. I *had* to keep my distance. But here? Against the idiots who live in *this* part of the house? The right words, spoken at just the right time, did the trick."

"It would have been nice," she said, "if you'd told us you were around, so we wouldn't have felt like we were doing this all by ourselves."

"It would have been," Mr. Notes's shadow agreed, "but what good would that have done? Can you imagine my telling you 'I'm here to help, but, oh, by the way, I can't do very much'? How would that have made you feel any better?"

Fernie wanted to stay mad, but couldn't come up with any good answers to that, and so stayed mad while feeling bad about it. "I don't suppose you can tell us where to find the Nightmare Vault."

"See?" Mr. Notes's shadow said petulantly. "That's exactly the kind of thing I was talking about. I don't have the slightest clue where to find it."

Fernie said, "I should have expected that."

"In fact, I'm not entirely sure that you should even be looking for it, since anything you find the shadow eater can find. If it were up to me, I'd look for it in places where I knew it was not."

Fernie wanted to scream with frustration. "You make it sound like the best we can do is run from him *forever*!"

"It is better than running toward him and being eaten up right away," Mr. Notes's shadow pointed out.

"Not by *much*," Fernie declared. "A life spent running away from things is no life at all!"

"Most rabbits would disagree with you."

The corridor came to a dead end with a vault door made of a completely round expanse of stained wood that, judging from the pattern of concentric rings, might have been the carved cross section of a tree not cut down until it was older than most major cities. The closest thing to a doorknob was a grasping iron hand at its precise center, inviting somebody to clasp it even though its fingernails were long and ragged and sharp enough to slice anybody who tried. Wisps of black mist puffed through the crack at the bottom of the door.

Gothic lettering across the door read:

WARNING
DO NOT ENTER
Hall of Shadow Criminals Within

Gustav reached for the grasping hand, but pulled back at the last moment. Sweat beads dotted his pale little forehead. "Fernie? You've met kind shadows. You've met mean ones. You've even met a few that were no help at all."

"That's harsh," Mr. Notes's shadow objected.

Gustav ignored him. "The shadows you'll meet behind this door are evil. They've been locked up because of terrible crimes against both shadows and people. You shouldn't get any closer to the cages than I do, and you shouldn't talk to anybody inside them unless I say it's all right. This is as bad as it gets. Okay?"

Fernie gulped. "Okay."

Gustav clasped the clawed hand, which immediately closed on his. The ragged claws cut his pale skin in several places, but he seemed to expect that and did not cry out in pain. After a moment the hand released his and a deep rumbling began. It was the sound of machinery doing whatever it had been designed to do after it had been left alone for a long time and was no longer quite certain that it could. It whined to let the two children and Mr. Notes's shadow know just how much it resented the task that had been asked of it.

Then the door rolled out of the way.

A gray mist spilled from the threshold, covering the floor at Fernie's feet to ankle depth.

"Stay close," Gustav warned her, just before taking the first step into the darkness.

Fernie had never been to a human prison, but she'd seen pictures and movies and had imagined a dim hall lined with stacked rows of tiny barred cells, all housing grim-faced men with neck tattoos and bad shaves.

That's not what the Hall of Shadow Criminals was like.

It was a vast indoor space as large as a stadium, but it gave the impression of a cramped dungeon, down to the thin streams of water dripping from a ceiling high enough to qualify as a sky. The floor was a labyrinth of narrow stone walkways hanging unsupported over a darkness that went down as far as Fernie could see.

"Don't step off the stone path," Gustav warned. "You'll fall all the way to the Dark Country."

Fernie tried not to look down. "Why do you have a special room with a pit that leads there if a shadow who wants to get there can just jump off one of these instead?"

Mr. Notes's shadow said, "Because the Dark Country is a big place, and anybody going down there on purpose wants to land in a place they could survive. Jump here instead of the Pit and I promise you, you won't. It's like the difference between walking out the door of your house and finding yourself in a familiar, friendly place like your front yard and falling off the deck of a ship and landing in the middle of a freezing ocean a thousand miles from the nearest beach." He hesitated, then added, "Plus, there are sharks."

"In the Dark Country or on the way down?"

"Both," Gustav said.

"Wonderful," Fernie muttered. She didn't

fall back into her habit of telling Gustav that his house was stupid, but she did think it.

As they moved deeper into the room, Fernie saw that the twisty stone paths surrounded a number of floating stone islands, each bearing a single tiny cell that looked like a cube made out of light. As far as she could tell, there were about twenty cubes in all, some visibly darkened by the silhouette of a solitary prisoner.

Some of those prisoners pounded on the walls. Some sat on the floors of their cells and shook in what seemed to be despair. A few paced restlessly, growing more agitated as the kids and Mr. Notes passed by, a lot like caged tigers planning for the day when the doors were left open and they were freed to make a fine lunch of raw zoo visitors.

After a while, Fernie noticed that while the cages of light were solid on all sides, one side was more transparent than the others, although it was still bright enough to keep its shadow criminal imprisoned. Most of the prisoners she could see looked as evil and cruel as their plight would have suggested. They hunched over and leered and brandished hands with fingernails like steak knives.

But then, at one point, having fallen a little bit behind Gustav and Mr. Notes's shadow because the path was narrow and she wanted to be sure of every step she took, Fernie found herself alone when one called out to her in the voice of a little girl. "Please, miss! Help me!"

Fernie knew that she shouldn't listen, but was stricken by the innocence in the caged shadow's voice. When she turned her head to look, she saw the occupant of the nearest cage, who seemed to be the shadow of a young girl with pigtails and wide, imploring eyes. "Please, miss! You look so pretty and kind! You can't leave me here! It's so lonely!"

Fernie's heart wouldn't let her walk away without saying anything. "I'm sorry. I can't help you."

The little girl shadow wailed and pressed closer to the wall of her cell. "No! Wait! Miss! Don't go away!"

Fernie cast a sad look at Gustav Gloom and Mr. Notes's shadow, who were about thirty steps ahead of her and concentrating on the path.

"I'm sorry, miss," the prisoner said quickly, "but I see that you don't cast a shadow. Did you lose yours?"

Fernie saw no reason to lie. "Yes."

"That's a sad and terrible thing, miss, because people in the world of light will find that strange and make fun of you. But it also means we might be able to help each other, because I don't have a person. I promise, if you release me, I'll stay with you and do everything you do, so you can live an ordinary life. Nobody will ever know."

Fernie was tempted. "You don't look anything like me. We would look strange to anybody who saw you following me around."

"But I could look like you, miss. That's an easy trick. Just look." The prisoner stretched and flexed and grew on all sides, and after a very few seconds became something that looked just like the shadow Fernie had lost. As she pressed her face against the clear wall of her cell, she even took on Fernie's own features, becoming a gray image recognizable down to the freckles. "See? Now I'm as pretty as you, I am. And all you have to do is come over here and place your hand on my cage."

Fernie thought about it. "That's pretty tempting."

The prisoner squealed. "Oh, thank you, miss! I knew you'd be nice! Please, come over here and we'll be friends, forever and ever."

The cage was just a short detour away. If Fernie wanted to do what the prisoner suggested, she could get away with it without either of her companions ever suspecting. She went so far as to put one foot on the path leading up to the prisoner's cage before pulling it back, tilting her head, and saying, "Hmmm."

"Hmmm what, miss?"

"I just had a little thought."

The prisoner appeared distressed. "Is something bothering you?"

"A lot of things are bothering me," Fernie said truthfully. "I've had a long night, I'm worried about my family, I'm tired of running around scared, and I no longer have a shadow."

"I would love to help you, miss."

"Yes." Fernie sighed. "I know. I could use another friend. But, this *one* thing . . ."

"You can tell me, miss. I won't be unkind."

Fernie said, "If you started out looking like one girl's shadow and could change yourself to look like another girl's shadow, how can I possibly know what you really look like, and what you really are?"

The prisoner was silent for a long time

before answering, this time in a voice that never could have belonged to any little girl: a voice older and deeper and more filled with menace than any voice Fernie had ever heard. *"Let me out now, you stupid little brat."*

It was not the voice of anything that should ever be allowed to run free.

Fernie shivered. "That was dumb of you. You might have still been able to talk me into it. But now, at least, I know for sure."

The prisoner, who swelled still further and was now more a hulking, threatening man than a bereft little girl, shouted angry curses at Fernie's back as she hurried up the path to where it next turned, and then to where it turned after that.

A few minutes later, she caught up to Gustav and Mr. Notes's shadow, who had noticed her absence and were heading back to make sure she was all right.

"You've got to keep up with us," Gustav complained. "What were you doing back there?"

"I'm sorry," Fernie apologized, shuddering as she glanced over her shoulder at the glowing cage of light now safely in the distance behind her. She answered truthfully. "I thought I saw something, but it was just a trick of the light."

CHAPTER FOURTEEN
TALKING TO HAIR ON A MOUSE

They walked the stone paths for another twenty minutes or so, taking a long time to cross the chamber because of how many times the route doubled back on itself.

The path they traveled moved left and then right and then left and right again, like the line for a popular amusement park ride, as it wound them closer to the cage Gustav wanted.

Then he told them, "His name's Hieronymus."

Fernie had never heard that name, which to her sounded like a strange way to pronounce *hair on a mouse*. "Is that his first name or his last name?"

"His first name. His family name is Spector, but I don't call him that; it's too close to *specter*, which means *ghost*, and the very last thing I need when talking to Hieronymus is to call him anything that makes him more scary."

Fernie said, "Do you speak to him a lot?"

"We've had four conversations, all because I needed information and had no other choice. He knows things."

"Who is he?"

"He was once Grandpa Lemuel's best friend in the shadow world. He was the one who made the deal with Grandpa to make this a shadow house. That was before he turned out to be one of the most evil shadows who ever lived."

"What did he do?"

"We don't need to get into it right now. There are a million stories in this house, and not all of them have anything to do with us. Let's just say he's a very, very evil being . . . and a very cunning one."

The cell they wanted was the most isolated of the lot, occupying a stone island so far away from the others that they appeared as just distant dots of light. It was also, for some reason, twice as big and therefore twice as ominous as the others. Fernie thought that whatever crime he had committed must have been an awful one for him to not even be able to see his fellow prisoners, and that he must be very lonely. But she had already encountered one evil shadow tonight, and the closer she got to that glowing box, the more the back of her neck prickled at the thought of what Hieronymus Spector must have done to be considered even worse.

Mr. Notes's shadow said, "I'll stay here, if you don't mind. I'd rather not get any closer to this villain than I have to."

Fernie reflected that Mr. Notes's shadow sure did like to stay out of trouble.

But Gustav didn't seem to mind. "That's probably for the best. Stand guard here and we'll meet you on the way back."

Gustav and Fernie moved farther on down the path, which approached Hieronymus Spector's cage from behind. Just ahead, the stone path split, with one branch leading to the stone island with Hieronymus's cage and one continuing straight ahead into darkness.

The branch that led straight ahead was the last of the room's many stone paths. It extended into the distance, a white line leading farther than Fernie's eyes could possibly follow, with nothing but blackness surrounding it. The shadow-stuff to its left and right seemed to churn like a sea disturbed by unseen currents, some of it spilling over the path in waves. Fernie thought she could see darker shapes moving just under the surface: shapes with fins, sharp teeth, and great gaping jaws.

Gustav stopped Fernie just before taking the left turn to Hieronymus Spector's island. "Are you frightened?"

Fernie could hardly believe the question. "You ask me that now?"

"It's all right. You should be. Just don't get any closer to his cage than I do. He has powers the others don't have, and has been known to pull people in."

"Okay."

Fernie was not a girl who needed her hand held in scary places, but she offered Gustav her hand now. He seemed grateful to take it.

Hand in hand, they turned left, stepped onto the island, and approached the front of the cage.

She saw now why this cage of light was twice as large as any of the others. It contained one of the smaller cages, shoved up against the back of the cell. Hieronymus Spector was inside the smaller one, but seemed too large to be contained by it; parts of him spilled through the walls of light, only slightly diluted by them. They were angry black clouds that looked like thunderheads just before a storm.

The inner cage looked like it was falling apart, unable to contain the darkness Hieronymus commanded. Even the outer cage already seemed like it was chipping at the edges. Sometime soon, whoever maintained this prison would need to put both the little cage and the bigger one inside a still bigger cage before Hieronymus made a hole big enough to escape through; but just looking at the damage he had already done, Fernie doubted that even that would be enough to keep him from escaping eventually.

The shadow inside the smaller cage was that of a man with a square jaw and a high forehead, who did not seem imprisoned at all. If anything, he seemed patient, willing to wait for time to free him.

"Ahhhh," he said as Gustav and Fernie came into view. "If it isn't my old friend the halfsie boy. You must be in big trouble to venture as far as this part of the house. I haven't seen you for more than a year."

"I've been busy," Gustav said.

"I'm not surprised," Hieronymus replied. "As I told your true mother, when she came to me asking if there was anything that could be done to give you a normal life in the world outside, you are trapped here forever, and the shadow world will create any number of dangers to swallow up the boy it sees as a crime against nature. Those dangers will only get worse as you get older. Still, visiting your old friend Hieronymus before now would have been the *polite* thing to do."

"You're right," Gustav said. "I'm sorry."

"If nothing else, it would give me the chance to share more reminiscences of your departed true mother. The poor, poor girl; it's so tragic that you had to bear such a terrible loss a second time, after what happened to the woman who only *should have been* your mother. Interesting, isn't it, that the only thing they really had in common was *you*. Maybe you're just bad luck to anybody foolish enough to love you."

Fernie had never been the type to remain silent while her friends or really anyone was being bullied. "He's *not* bad luck! He's my best friend!"

Hieronymus seemed to see Fernie for the first time. "I hadn't gotten to you yet, girl. I see that you cast no shadow. Tell me, girl, did Nebuchadnezzar's shadow make you any special offers on the way in? Did he pretend to be a frightened little girl?"

Fernie thrust out her chin. "He didn't fool me. I didn't know that was his real name, but I knew he was something bad, and he didn't fool me. You don't fool me, either. You're just a bully in a cage who doesn't get to have any fun unless he's saying terrible things to people. But I'm not going to let you talk to Gustav that way."

The figure in the cage inside a cage tilted its head, as if amused by this. "And I should obey you why? I don't even know your name."

"My name's—"

Gustav put a cold hand on her arm, stopping her. "Don't. Just don't." He turned back to the prisoner. "This is between you and me, Hieronymus."

"Maybe I don't want to talk to you, hmmm? Maybe I'm mad at you for not visiting me for so long. Maybe I want to make new friends, somebody else who might be willing to visit me even when she doesn't need information."

Fernie almost retorted that she didn't want a friend as mean as Hieronymus Spector, anyway. But Gustav spoke before she could: "And maybe if you don't tell me what I need to know, I'll never come back and you'll lose the closest thing to a friend you *do* have. It's better to answer me.

What do you know about the Nightmare Vault?"

For the first time, Hieronymus sounded interested. "Oh-ho! Somebody's looking for *that* old thing again?"

"Somebody very dangerous is looking for it. We know what it looks like but not where it is or why it's so powerful."

Hieronymus Spector chuckled a little. "I'll only give the answer to that question to the poor girl without a shadow."

Gustav glanced at Fernie, who nodded at him. "Just don't give him your name."

She nodded to show Gustav she understood, then faced Hieronymus. "Talk."

"Do you go to school, little girl?"

"Of course I do. It's still summer vacation right now, but it starts back up in a couple of weeks."

"Do you read books?"

"Duh. Of course I read books. I'm not *stupid*."

"It would be wonderful for you not to be stupid, but I believe I'll be the judge of that. Have you ever heard the story of Pandora's box?"

Fernie had. "It's a myth, isn't it?"

"It's like many myths, little girl: a poorly remembered story from the hidden history of the world. What do you know of Pandora's box?"

Fernie resented being forced to perform. "The way the story goes, once upon a time life was perfect and all the awful troubles of the world, all the diseases and the wars and so on, were locked away in the box so they wouldn't bother people. Then this stupid girl named Pandora got curious about what was inside and opened the lid, letting them out."

"That's the story people tell, little girl," Hieronymus said. "But it's not what really happened; it's just the closest their little minds can come to understanding it."

Fernie rolled her eyes. "Maybe my mind's not as small as you think."

The dark clouds in the cage of light churned like smoke billowing from a fire. "And maybe it is, but I can explain it in words small enough to fit."

Fernie knew that she was supposed to be angered by this, so she said nothing.

"The world's always had troubles like, as you put it, 'all the diseases and the wars and so on.' But once there were even bigger problems: the creatures who lived at the dawn of time, before man, before dinosaurs, before even the stars, things so old and so terrible that they were never given names. They were terrible things, little girl . . . and though they all died, their shadows did not. They slept on, dreaming of the day when they'd take back what was once theirs. Long ago, before history, men and shadows worked together to gather up these dozing monsters and lock them up in a prison even more terrible than the one you see around you. To your eyes, little girl, that prison would resemble a small chest, about the size of a jewelry box. That is what your people now remember as Pandora's box, and it has never been opened, not in all the years from the dawn of history to now. If somebody's looking for it, he wants to wake those creatures and set them loose on the world."

Gustav nodded. "Why?"

"Because they would awake hungry, eat everything and everybody, then go far, far away in search of more food . . . thus leaving the world around us empty of life and ready to be taken by anybody else who wanted to fill it."

Fernie understood. She was sickened by it, but she understood. "It's . . . like knocking down a perfectly good old house so another one could be built in its place."

"Oh, you are a smart girl. That's right. Anybody who wants that box thinks he can tear down the world and put up a better one. Or, at least, one better for *him*."

Fernie thought she saw a flaw in the story. "But we've been told what the Nightmare Vault looks like, and it's much bigger than any old jewelry box."

"That's right. The box I describe is not the Nightmare Vault. For many years it was kept in a closely guarded chamber in the Dark Country, but then one day there was the latest in a long series of attempts to steal it . . . and the shadows guarding it grew afraid. So they asked me to ask Gustav's grandfather, who they'd come to trust, to hide it where no evil man or shadow would ever be able to find it."

Gustav's grim expression was even more grim now. "That's what Howard Philip October was looking for all those years ago."

Hieronymus Spector seemed downright delighted by that. "Is this about *him*?"

"In a way."

"He's back?"

Gustav hesitated. "In a way."

"How delightful! Do you know, I always

thought it would be great fun to let that teller of silly stories into the house and take bets on how long it took him to either find the Nightmare Vault or walk into the wrong room and get himself killed stupidly. But your grandfather had no sense of fun. He wanted nothing to do with anybody who would even think of releasing the shadows from before time."

With that last phrase, a cold breeze blew against Fernie's arms, raising goose bumps. She hugged herself, wished her father had been here to hug her, too, and looked back over the path they had traveled. The mazelike stone walkways stretched as far as her eyes could see, and so did the cages of solid light, even if they were just specks of light, like stars.

As she watched, one of the distant specks behind her flickered out.

She barely heard Gustav asking Hieronymus, "Do you know where my grandfather hid it?"

"I'm not sure I should tell you."

Gustav said, "I'm not going to open the box. I'm just going to hide it again."

"I don't care what you do. That's not the reason."

"What is, then?"

"Because," Hieronymus said peevishly, "I'm stuck in a cage, and it might actually be *fun* watching your world get eaten if the person you're trying to hide it from gets to it before you do."

Another of the distant spots of light went out. Fernie took a step closer to the edge of the stone island and peered out into the distance, her heart pounding as she tried to figure out what was happening.

Gustav asked Hieronymus, "But what if he doesn't find it? What if the world doesn't get eaten and I get so mad at you for not helping me that I don't ever come back and visit you again?"

Hieronymus said, "That's a thought. I should give you *something*, just to keep matters interesting."

Another spot of light went out. Fernie squinted and found that she could just barely make out movement: a churning, angry *darkness* between them and the exit that was moving closer with every second. She peered around the side of Hieronymus's cage and saw Mr. Notes's shadow racing toward her in terror.

Behind her, Hieronymus told Gustav, "The thing is, I didn't see your grandfather hide it. I only know what he told me."

Three of the distant lights went out.

Fernie said, "Gustav."

"It's important for you to understand that this isn't *exactly* what he told me," Hieronymus said. "He seemed to say that he still had to think the matter over."

"That's all he said?" Gustav pressed.

"He didn't say *that* at all. Just something like that. Something that meant that."

One of the few cells close enough to look like a cell and not like a distant speck of light started to flicker at the edges. A black line, like ink from an invisible pen, drew itself across the glowing box, cutting it in half. Another came down over the first line, cutting it in half again. Then the edges started crumbling, as if being nibbled by invisible mice.

Fernie suddenly realized what she was looking at: swirling tendrils of shadow, blocking her view of the cages as their master drew closer. "Gustav!"

Before she could yell, Hieronymus said, "Of course . . . if October happens this way . . . just to keep matters interesting, I'll be sure to give him more *helpful* directions."

Fernie couldn't take it anymore. Nor could Mr. Notes's shadow. Girl and shadow both cried out—in the girl's case at the top of her lungs, in the shadow's case at the top of whatever it was he used for lungs.

"Gustav! October's found us!"

CHAPTER FIFTEEN
BETRAYED BY HAIR ON A MOUSE

They ran.

It wasn't the first time that they'd had to run for their lives from a writhing mass of jet-black tendrils. Most houses don't require visitors to do that kind of thing even once, let alone thrice; it just isn't the kind of situation that ever comes up anywhere else.

They couldn't run back in the direction they'd come, not with October blocking the way, so they had to use the last of the stone walkways, the one that stretched out into the unseen distance, with nothing but a bottomless plunge into darkness on both sides.

Fernie yelled, "Where does *this* lead?"

"I don't know!" Gustav yelled back. "I've never been out any farther than Hieronymus Spector's cell!"

The path wasn't wide enough for them

to run side by side, so they ran in single file, Gustav just an arm's reach ahead of Fernie. Mr. Notes's shadow flew through the air over both, neither following nor leading, just keeping up, in what could have been either protectiveness or a desire to be protected. He kept saying, "Oh dear, oh dear, oh dear."

With the path so narrow and the threat of slipping over the side so disastrous, none of them bothered to look over their shoulders to see if October was gaining; they just kept running, hoping to eventually arrive somewhere useful.

Unfortunately, the farther they went, the less reliable the section of stone path became; it began to look more and more ragged at the edges, marked by rough spots wherever pieces of stone had chipped off. The churning sea of darkness on both sides became rougher, too, with more and more ripples of shadow spilling over the sides and covering the stone, like surf reclaiming a sunken pier.

"I'm not sure how much farther we can go!" Fernie cried.

"I know!" Gustav yelled. "I don't think there is anything out here—just empty space, kept in case there are any more prisoners!"

Then the stone path dipped below the surface of the shadow sea. Gustav plunged into darkness up to his knees, billowing up all around him as he continued to stumble in the same direction, only barely slowing down. Fernie sank in up to her knees, too, shrieking as she thought of the sharks Gustav had mentioned. She slowed down, too, long enough to turn around and see if October was still coming—and yes, there he was: a distant, lumpy man-shape bobbing along at the center of the storm of tendrils originating from his open mouth.

Mr. Notes's shadow stared at the sight. "I'd offer to give up my life to slow him down, but I don't think I could slow him down."

"Don't bother," Gustav said as he continued to run on the submerged path. "You wouldn't."

Mr. Notes's shadow said, "I could tell him I know where to find the Nightmare Vault. It would be a lie, but I could tell him that."

Fernie shook her head. "I already told him that earlier tonight."

Gustav whirled in place. "Really? Even *I* didn't tell him that. I just told him I'd look for it."

"I needed him to chase me instead of chasing Pearlie."

"That would do it," Gustav said. He took another step farther onto the path and sank another three feet, his head immediately vanishing from sight. The black mist over his head churned a little harder, as if from the struggles of a little boy fighting to surface.

Fernie cried out and almost leaped in after him. "He's drowning!"

Mr. Notes's shadow blocked her way. "It's not *water*, Fernie. It's more like a thick fog. You've been in places like that and still been able to breathe, right?"

"But there are sharks in there!"

"Right now," Mr. Notes's shadow said, "I think we have bigger problems."

Unwillingly, Fernie looked where Mr. Notes's shadow pointed. Not nearly far enough behind them, the gaining form of Howard Philip October had turned back. The cloud of black tendrils carrying him had retreated inside his mouth, leaving him to stride on his own two feet back to a place he'd already passed: the glowing cage of Hieronymus Spector.

He stepped onto Spector's island and tilted his head slightly, listening to what the imprisoned shadow had to say.

Fernie felt a pang of fear. "Hieronymus is telling him everything he told us."

"I'm afraid it's worse than that," Mr. Notes's shadow said. "If I know Hieronymus, he's doing what he promised and telling October *more* than he told you."

Fernie's fear became something much worse: the end of all hope. She hadn't stopped October or saved her sister and father; she'd failed so badly that the end of the entire world was coming. Before long the shadows of ancient monsters would run loose, and everything good would be swept aside for the new kingdom Lord Obsidian wanted to build.

Visible again now that October had pulled the shadow tendrils back in, the sprawling maze of stone paths and the distant glowing cages of Hieronymus's fellow prisoners all seemed to blur as the tears welled in Fernie's eyes.

Then a voice behind her said, "What's wrong?"

She whirled back around and saw Gustav standing in waist-deep shadow-stuff. Puffs of black mist, disturbed when he surfaced, slowly sank on all sides, like soap bubbles.

From his expression, he had no idea whatsoever why Fernie would be crying.

Mr. Notes's shadow said, "Hieronymus is telling October where to find the Nightmare Vault."

Gustav didn't seem disturbed by that at all. "Yes. He said he was going to."

Fernie cried, "We've got to stop him!"

Gustav seemed curious. "Who's *him* in that sentence? Are we supposed to stop Hieronymus from telling October where to find it, or October from rushing off to get it?"

Fernie didn't understand why he was so calm. "Both!"

Gustav looked past her, to Hieronymus's island, where the discussion between the ice-cream man and the traitor shadow seemed to have ended. October had sprouted his tendrils again and was allowing them to carry him back in the opposite direction.

Gustav shook his head. "I'm sorry, but Hieronymus has already said everything he's going to say, and October's already on his way to get the Nightmare Vault. So we're too late to stop either one of those things. Would you settle for getting there first and saving the world?"

Fernie said, "What?"

Gustav addressed Mr. Notes's shadow. "I'm

sorry, but if you follow us under the mists, you'll probably just attract sharks, and I'd rather you didn't. Is it okay if I ask you to just find your own way out?"

Mr. Notes's shadow seemed torn between loyalty to Gustav and relief at being spared any dangerous encounters with sharks. "Should I meet you in the grand parlor?"

Fernie cried, *"What?"*

"If we're not there in an hour," Gustav told Mr. Notes's shadow, "it's because we got killed."

Gustav's shadow friend nodded. "That's what I would have figured, anyway."

Fernie's mouth opened and closed and opened and closed. "What? What? *What!?*"

Gustav glanced at her, and though he didn't smile with his lips, there was a hint of one in his eyes. "Well, come along, then."

He strode down the path until his head disappeared under the gray waves of shadow-stuff.

Fernie had time for one last worry about being eaten by sharks before the urgency of the moment took over and she had to follow, running where she would have preferred not to go at all.

She almost shrieked and turned back as the path dipped beneath her feet and the shadow-stuff rose over her head, but Mr. Notes's shadow had told the truth: Despite the promise of sharks and the surface that behaved like waves on an ocean, the darker regions into which she had plunged were not very much like water after all. They were just gray mists, a shade darker and sootier than what she'd been passing through before. Walking through them didn't feel any worse than being in the shadow of a wall that stood between herself and the sun. As long as there was still a stone path beneath her feet, walking in the stuff was not very uncomfortable at all.

It was far spookier, though. There was nothing to see but the path itself, a dim straight line at her feet, as it headed downward into the murk . . . that, and the faraway black shapes of finned, toothy creatures who looked very much like sharks, swimming in the shadow-stuff the way the ones she had seen at the aquarium swam in water. There seemed to be an awful lot of them, and they weren't nearly far away enough to suit her.

Gustav was twenty steps ahead, not running

but walking very fast, his arms pumping with determination.

It only took her a second to catch up. "Why won't you tell me what's going on? Didn't you hear me say *What?* all those times?"

He kept walking. "Yes, I did. I thought it was odd, but I can cry out my last name, too. Gloom! Gloom! Gloom!"

The realization that he was teasing her at such a serious moment made her furious. *"Gustav—"*

He cut her off. "Do you still have the glass globe I gave you? I still have mine."

Fernie had been carrying it all along, though it had been long minutes since she'd bothered to think of it. "Yes. Can I ask you a question?"

"You ask me questions all the time."

"Why aren't we running?"

"There's no point. We're not being chased at the moment. And we don't want to slip and fall over the side, not here and not now; not considering what's at stake, how far we'd fall, and the terrible part of the Dark Country where we'd land. Just keep moving. I saw an exit not far ahead."

She supposed it didn't matter all that much whether they were walking or running, not when

Gustav was walking faster than most people could run. So she did her best to keep up, shivering a little when she saw a host of darker shapes gliding by in the mists. "What about the sharks?"

"Them? I never said they were dangerous to *us*. There are worse ones, farther down, but the ones swimming near the surface are only dangerous to shadows. That's why I told Mr. Notes's shadow not to come with us; they would have eaten *him* right up. Us, they won't even bother—especially since neither one of us has a shadow right now and don't even *smell* good to them."

Now that Fernie looked, the dark shapes swarming about in the mists did seem to be keeping their distance. "But what about—"

"Sorry," Gustav said. "It's my turn. I get to ask you one."

"Come on! You haven't explained anything yet!"

"Sorry," he said. "It's still my turn. I wanted to ask you about what you told Hieronymus. About my being your best friend."

She couldn't believe he wanted to talk about that *now*. "Come on, Gustav. You know we're friends."

"Oh, I knew we were friends, but I didn't know we were *best* friends. Is that true?"

"Why would you believe it wasn't?"

"It's just surprising," he said, "because it makes sense for *you* to be *my* best friend. I'm stuck behind the estate gates and haven't met a lot of people. Any friend I made, even a bad one, would still be my *best* friend, just because there's nothing else she could be. But you . . . you're out in the world. You've been to school. You must have known a *hundred* kids in your life. Am I really *your* best friend?"

"Don't be stupid," she said irritably. It had only been two weeks since she'd introduced him to her sister as "*by far* the coolest friend I've ever had," which as far as she was concerned meant the same thing. "*Of course* you are."

He fell into silence as they hurried down the slanting stone path, which wound through shadowy murk among the shadowy sharks beyond the shadow prison in the most shadowy place of his shadowy house.

He remained silent even as a small mote of light appeared up ahead and grew larger as they approached, revealing itself as a portal to a brighter place.

The path through the Gloom house's darkest places led straight back to hope, after all.

CHAPTER SIXTEEN
A FINE SUMMER DAY IN OCTOBER

Gustav and Fernie passed through the portal and found a little set of curving stone stairs, which led upward through a murk already far lighter than anything they'd been passing through for some time. When they ran up those stairs and emerged into what would be considered dry land if they'd been traveling through water, a circular vault door at the top slid aside to reveal a dingy hallway identical to the one that had led to the shadow prison in the first place, except reversed.

Even the warning on the door was reversed:

WARNING
DO NOT ENTER
Hall of Shadow Criminals Within

"It looks like the other side of the same door," Fernie said.

Even Gustav was impressed. "I think in some way it may even *be* the same door. I think, in a way, the entire prison may be *in* the door. Either way . . . we really do need to run now."

Fernie had spent more time running in this house than anywhere else, so this was hardly a surprise.

They ran.

They ran through corridors dim and dingy, through rooms grim and gruesome.

They ran around corners, up stairs, and through a freestanding wardrobe. They ran down a hallway with a crumbling gap in the middle, with nothing but wreckage and shadow-stuff below them, and though she would have liked to stop and judge the leap, Gustav said there was no time, so they jumped the gap and moved on.

At a wall covered with a painting of a very serious man with a mustache so ornate that it must have taken him half his day to comb it, they paused just long enough for Gustav to open the painting like a door and reveal a hidden doorway to the servants' passage.

Fernie still couldn't tell one part of that twisty maze from another, but Gustav could, seeing some pattern in the thin corridors that she could not. As they raced up and down stairs and along narrow passages in the space behind the walls of the Gloom house, she began to realize that wherever he was leading them, they were getting close.

Then they burst from the servants' passage onto a green carpet and both fell to their knees, for the moment too exhausted from all their running to take as much as one more step.

For the first time since leaving the Hall of Shadow Criminals, Fernie knew exactly where they'd been going. She gasped in recognition. "The house . . . inside the house?"

It was indeed the room where Lemuel Gloom had built a cozy home for his family; the room where the glowing ball of sunlight still shone over the slanting roof of the smaller house where Hans and Penelope Gloom had wanted to live.

They both panted for almost a full minute before Gustav forced himself back upright. "I . . . don't think . . . we have much time . . . before he gets here. We have to . . . hurry."

"But . . . Gustav . . . are you sure it's *here*? In your family's *house*?"

"It . . . makes sense," he managed as he dragged her to her feet. "Anything . . . that dangerous . . . Grandpa Lemuel would want to keep nearby . . . where he could keep an eye on it . . . and stop anybody bad, man or shadow, from trying to take it. It wouldn't . . . have been . . . *safe* . . . anywhere else."

"But, Gustav . . . how can you *know* . . . ?"

Gustav didn't answer, maybe because he didn't have time to answer. Instead he left her behind and ran into the house inside the house, the rear door slamming. She stumbled after him and found him in the empty kitchen as he wrapped a sheet of aluminum foil around his glass globe.

"Gustav—"

"There's no time . . . to explain," he said. He had already gotten his breathing most of the way under control and sounded only a little ragged as he wrapped the globe, except for the one open end, in silvery sheets. "It took longer than . . . I expected to get here and . . . I think he'll . . . be on us any second. I think he'll be coming from the front yard. You need . . . to go out into the front yard . . . under the sun, and watch for him. Shout if you see him coming. Slow him down if you can."

The idea of having to stand still and wait as October approached was so against every instinct in Fernie's body that she never would have agreed to do it for anybody other than Gustav. She nodded and headed for the front of the house.

"Wait," he said.

She turned, expecting him to wish her good luck.

"Your globe," he said.

She looked down at her right hand, which still held the globe he had handed her. She'd never put it down, not in all the adventures that followed. Without a word she placed it on the table beside him and began to leave again.

"Wait," he said.

She looked at him.

"Thank you for calling me your best friend," he said.

"Thanks for being my best friend," she replied.

She turned and once again headed for the front of the house.

"Wait," he said a third time.

She turned around and looked at him.

"Good luck," he said.

"You too," she said.

She bounded out onto the front lawn.

It felt strange to be directly under a sun again after so many hours of running around the dark corridors of Gustav's house, and especially after their adventures in the shadow prison. She could only hope that it wasn't the last sun she ever got to see, and that she would have another chance to be warmed by the more distant and yet somehow friendlier sun from the world outside.

The thought made her feel more alone than ever before. Though there was a sun blazing away just over her head, she felt a terrible cold that could not have been matched during the most frigid snowstorm in January.

Then something landed on her head with a plop.

She yelled and fought a heroic battle with her attacker that would have had the greatest warriors of all time nodding with appreciation and carefully taking notes, until she managed to get out from under it and saw that it was just a dusty old sheet, covered with a pattern of roses.

"Sorry!" cried Gustav, who had tossed it out the nursery window. "I didn't mean for it to land on you! Spread it out on the lawn!"

Fernie had no idea why Gustav would want her to do such a thing, with the air around her already growing cold from October's approach, but assumed that he had his reasons. She spread the king-sized sheet across the fake lawn, and just because it was something to do took extra care to make sure that all the wrinkles were smoothed out.

Then she stood up and faced the door she had followed Gustav through just before her first visit with the green carpet pretending to be a lawn. On this side of the wall, it was just the outline of a door, painted with the same mural of bright blue skies and faraway rolling hills as the rest of the wall around it. She could almost close her eyes and imagine that the fake horizon was real. But no, it was only a painting. That peaceful horizon was just a made-up thing, less real than the danger that was coming for them.

When she heard distant crunching, the sound October's tendrils of darkness had made as they punched holes through the balcony over the grand parlor, it took every ounce of courage she had to resist running for her life.

Her teeth chattered before she clamped her jaw shut.

Then a hole appeared in the wall before her. A black tendril poked through, seemed to look around a bit, and then retreated, as if to report to its master what it had seen. Another half dozen tendrils crashed through the wall, ripping apart the fake hills and fake clouds and fake beautiful summer day as if offended that anybody would ever decorate their home with such things. October hadn't caused such damage the last time he'd entered this room, but he seemed to be in a greater hurry this time now that he knew his prize was so near. The frustration he must have felt after his last encounter with Gustav and Fernie must have also lent fury to his dark mission.

The door blew off its frame.

A formless, swirling mass spilled out into the room where Fernie stood, curling around the doorway and slithering across the fake grass like an army of black snakes. October followed close behind, floating a foot off the floor as the shadow tendrils carried him along, like a package they'd been asked to deliver.

Gustav had asked Fernie to let him know when October showed up, so she felt absolutely no shame about screaming at the very sight. But she might have screamed anyway. This was the first time she had seen October up close since helping Gustav drop the big gong on his head, so it was also the first time she could see the effects of the impact. His head looked like a flat clay sculpture that somebody had stepped on; his features had flattened, turning his nose into an outline against the planes of his cheeks. His skin was black-and-blue, and his eyes hung askew, no longer lined up perfectly like eyes should be, but one mashed farther down his face by several inches. One of those eyes was open, the other puffy and closed.

His mouth, though . . . that was unchanged. That was still open, and still spilling out thickets of grasping black tendrils.

The man-shaped creature at the center of all that darkness stopped only a few steps into the room to peer at Fernie with dull curiosity as the shadowy tendrils he controlled spread out to fill every corner of the lawn. They encircled Fernie, weaving together until she was completely imprisoned in a cage of them.

Behind her, some of the snaky black shapes spilling through the open screen door of the house inside the house groped for whatever they expected to find within; others curled up to the open second-story window, invading the nursery. In seconds all she could see of the house was the sloping roof. She heard ransacking sounds as the search began.

The shadow eater didn't come any closer to her. He stared at her, tilting his flattened head first one way, then the other. "The girl who ran," he said in his dull, empty voice. "The girl who lied. The girl who helped to drop the big bell on my head. I told you that you would be punished if you didn't help me. Now we are back in the same room where we were hours ago, and all your running has come to nothing."

"I'm not sorry," Fernie said, her voice quavering only a little as she said it. She had been afraid, but she was past that now, ready for anything that might happen.

"You won't stop October from getting the Nightmare Vault."

"No. I won't. But you want to know something?"

The tendrils around her drew closer. "No."

"I'll tell you anyway," she said, speaking quickly because she only had seconds left. "I agree with something my friend Gustav said about you. I don't think you *are* Howard Philip October. I think you're just an empty, stupid *thing* that the real Howard Philip October made to fetch what he wants."

October was silent for several seconds, absorbing that . . . and then he said, "Being right won't save you."

Shadow tendrils whipped around Fernie's ankles, lifting her shrieking form off the ground and into the air.

The room's sun veered so close that she shut her eyes tight, afraid of being burned up; but though she was swung so close to that ball of fire that she could have reached out and touched it if she'd tried, she felt no heat at all except in her eyes, which though closed were momentarily dazzled by its brightness.

It was certainly better than what she saw when the grip of the tendrils swung her away from the sun and she opened her eyes to see the shadow eater's head, rolling back as his mouth opened wider and wider. There was nothing in there but empty space and more churning black shapes, some of them looking like the shadows of people.

She closed her eyes so she wouldn't have to watch as October swallowed her whole.

But that's when Gustav yelled, *"Oh no, you don't!"*

Fernie had been so terrified that she'd forgotten all about Gustav, but when she opened her eyes again she spotted him swinging from shadow tendril to shadow tendril like a monkey swinging among vines in the jungle. He didn't seem afraid at all: just angry, and determined, and so much in control of the situation that, for a heartbeat, he seemed as fearsome as the shadow eater himself.

When he passed between her and the room's sun, like an eclipse in the shape of a boy, she saw two brilliant points of light, burning at the center of his chest. They were the glass globes he had insisted on collecting earlier, each now wrapped in aluminum foil and clanking together in a sling he had made of another wadded-up bedsheet from the house. The open ends of both glass globes glowed from the fires burning inside them—fire made of the pure burning daylight he had just scooped from the surface of the room's sun.

For the first time, Fernie began to understand the nature of Gustav's plan, something she never could have imagined herself, because she never would have dared dream that it was possible.

Forgotten in the shadow eater's grip, the way her father sometimes forgot he was carrying his car keys because he was too busy concentrating on bigger problems, Fernie could only watch as every tendril that had invaded the house inside the house suddenly pulled back out to dart in Gustav's direction at once. It was like watching a thousand spears, thrown by a thousand warriors, all angrily converging on the same boy.

It looked hopeless for Gustav, but then he appeared, somehow leaping past that storm of darkness without ever being touched by it, running across a bucking bridge of groping darkness toward the shadow eater's gaping mouth. Gustav had one of the glass globes in his hand and was winding up to throw it. But then the tendrils thrashed, and he dropped the globe; it fell past the thicket of swirling darkness to the fake grass and shattered, releasing a blinding burst of light that dissipated some of the invading darkness but didn't come even close to stopping the shadow eater.

But that was why Gustav had packed two globes. He needed a spare.

Even as a thousand grasping tendrils reached for him again, he grabbed the remaining globe and dove straight into the shadow eater's open mouth.

Fernie shrieked. It was that terrible. It looked exactly like the boy she'd called her best friend was being eaten.

But her shriek was not nearly as loud as the shadow eater's. He threw back his head and bellowed, shafts of light pouring from a gaping mouth that until now had only emitted darkness. An army of dark shapes, driven from his belly by that light, flew out, all of them adding to the chorus of screams; all of the ones the fake October had eaten, that had been in his power before, now had to follow their nature and flee something that always drove shadows before it. There were more of them than Fernie ever could have imagined: not just hundreds of them but thousands, many of them crying "Free! Free!" as they escaped into the open air.

The tendrils holding Fernie by the ankles released her. She fell toward the ground, shutting her eyes again as she braced for the impact. But it never came. Other shadows, freed by Gustav's brave act, caught her and gently lowered her to the fake lawn. One said, "I'm sorry we can't stay to help, but we still have to get as far away from that monster as we can," and joined the many others fleeing through the holes the shadow eater had ripped in the walls.

Fernie didn't mind. She only cared about Gustav.

Unhurt, in the center of what looked like a tornado of swirling light and darkness, she rose to her feet and watched October deflate like a punctured tire. The more shadows escaped him, the more saggy and wrinkly and flat he became, until he was revealed as the only thing he'd ever been: an empty sack of skin, filled with the shadows he had stolen.

The top of Gustav's head emerged from that gaping, boneless mouth. More of Gustav's body appeared as what was left of the shadow eater sank lower and lower around him, until all that was left was Gustav standing in a now-rumpled black suit and the deflated shadow eater bunched around his ankles, like a pair of pajama bottoms Gustav hadn't gotten around to kicking aside yet.

Fernie cried out. "Gustav! I can't believe you beat him!"

"That's because I haven't," Gustav said.

"B-but—"

"He might not look like much now, but as soon as the last of the sunshine inside him spills out, he'll be able to start swallowing shadows again. If we don't do something to stop him from doing that, he'll fill up again in no time. It'd only take him a few days to get back to being every bit as dangerous as he was."

Fernie gave the sack of empty skin a worried glance. Did October's eyes roll a little toward her, like marbles in that fleshy, empty face? Did that face look a little less flat, a little bit more like the monster he had been only a few seconds ago?

She gulped and stepped away. "What'll we do?"

"Don't be silly," Gustav said. "What do you think I tossed you the bedsheet for?"

He picked up the empty, loose sack that the shadow eater had become and carried him, dangling streamerlike arms, yellowish uniform and all, to the sheet Fernie had laid out on the lawn. He dumped the empty monster in the middle of the sheet and started curling up the edges.

"You've got to be kidding me," Fernie said. "How can it possibly be that simple?"

"He's a shadow eater," Gustav said. "He's only as powerful as the number of shadows he can capture. Keep him wrapped up somewhere he can't have any shadows to eat and he's just an empty sack of nothing that can't even stand up by itself."

But then, just before he covered up the shadow eater's face, Gustav hesitated, and asked him, "You might as well tell me: Where's the real October?"

The empty lips flapped. "In . . . the Dark Country . . ."

"Is he with Lord Obsidian?"

"Yes . . ."

Gustav hesitated. "Is *he* Lord Obsidian?"

"Yes . . ."

"And my father? Where's my father?"

"He's there, too . . . a prisoner . . . beyond your reach . . . forever."

Gustav's habitual frown became a fierce scowl. "We'll see about that."

He resumed wrapping. Within minutes, he

had a nice tight bundle, all tied in a knot.

"There," he said, and glanced down at Fernie's feet. "One secured shadow eater. Now that he's harmless, you've even got your shadow back."

Fernie looked down and saw that Gustav was right. Where her feet touched the ground, Fernie's shadow sat protectively circling her legs. She didn't look much like Fernie right now, but then, she wouldn't; not with the indoor sun hovering right overhead, making her most comfortable as a little patch of darkness at Fernie's feet. Even so, Fernie was delighted to see her. "Thanks for helping me back at the house."

"It was nothing," her shadow said. "Thanks for helping Gustav free me from that smelly pig."

They went back inside the house inside the house, which was, in the aftermath of the battle, no longer the nice family home that Lemuel Gloom had built and that Hans and Penelope Gloom had known. The shadow eater's tendrils had shattered furniture and poked hundreds of holes in the walls. Entire steps had been ripped out of the staircase leading to the second floor.

Fernie didn't think the structure would remain standing for long, but Gustav said that it would be all right for now and that he would see to it that repairs were made. He led her upstairs and carried the bundle imprisoning the shadow eater into the master bedroom, which was covered with dust from holes tendrils had poked in the ceiling, but had otherwise escaped the very worst of the damage.

As Gustav began to climb the ladder to the ridiculously tall bed, Fernie tried to show him that she had everything all figured out. "It's the bed, right? The Nightmare Vault, I mean."

"Not quite," Gustav said as he reached the top of the ladder and shoved the mattress to one side. "It's actually *under* the bed. Grandpa must have built the bed around it, because he wanted to guard it himself and wanted to make sure nobody else could get to it while he slept."

"How long have you known?"

"Since Hieronymus told me."

"I heard everything Hieronymus told you, and I don't remember his telling you that."

"You weren't paying enough attention. He said, 'I didn't see your grandfather hide it. I only know what he told me.' And then he said that my grandfather had 'seemed to say' he needed to think the matter over."

Fernie remembered all that. "So?"

"So," Gustav said, "my grandfather didn't *actually* say that he had to think it over. He just *seemed to say* that he had to think it over. I just had to think of something he could have said that could have meant, 'I'm going to think it over,' while really meaning something quite different."

Fernie honestly didn't get it. "What did he really say?"

"In a minute. Come up and take a look at this."

Fernie climbed up the ladder and saw the sliding panel the mattress had hidden. Gustav opened it, revealing a large empty space, and below it, a massive antique chest lying on its back, its handles bound together with heavy chains. It was impossible not to think about the terrible Nightmare Vault, the dangerous creatures imprisoned inside it, and how close October had come to freeing them.

Gustav dropped the tightly wrapped bundle containing the shadow eater through the open panel. It flopped on top of the chest and sat there, where it might stay forever, its own monster as imprisoned by a bedsheet as the monsters inside the Nightmare Vault were imprisoned.

"I even kept my promise to him," Gustav said as he shut the panel and once again shifted the mattress over it. "I did bring him to the Nightmare Vault."

Fernie still burned with the need to know. "What did your grandfather really *say*?"

The answer was one of Gustav's very rare smiles. It was not a happy smile, like the one he'd flashed on his first taste of a chocolate chip cookie, but it was a satisfied one, in its own way one of the scariest expressions Fernie had ever seen.

"He said he was going to sleep on it."

CHAPTER SEVENTEEN
GUSTAV'S MOTHER

As they made their way out, so relieved that the danger was over that they talked about anything but what they'd been through, they saw signs of the shadows returning to the Gloom house.

The bubbling gray mist that usually covered every room to ankle height and that had been missing most places that Gustav and Fernie had been began to roll out again; the dark shapes began to reappear, wandering on their various errands again; the dim, forlorn wreck the house had seemed to be with the shadows gone gave way to the dark, magical place Fernie had remembered, with floating figures and silent presences drifting by everywhere.

None seemed eager to thank Gustav for saving them. When Fernie expressed irritation at this, he shrugged. "Why would they? Most of these aren't the shadows I know, the ones like Great-Aunt Mellifluous who raised me; they aren't even the ones I've lived with all my life. These are the ones who were imprisoned inside the shadow eater, the ones he stole from all over the world before coming here in search of the Vault. Mine will be back later, as soon as they learn it's safe to come out of hiding. It's probably going to be a lot more crowded here for a while, until the others get around to going back to wherever they were when the shadow eater captured them."

"It's still not fair," Fernie protested. "They owe you."

"Shadows aren't always fair," Gustav said. And then, before she had a chance to say anything, he added, "Few things in life are."

It would take her a while to realize how sadly he'd said that.

When they reached the front door, Fernie hesitated a moment before it would have opened for her. She realized that Gustav was no longer at her side. She turned around and saw that he'd walked away and was now just a tiny figure at the end of the hallway, returning to the strange places where he'd spent so much of his life. Though the familiar form of Mr. Notes's shadow now stood next to him, no boy had ever looked sadder or more alone.

She almost went after him, but it had been a long and nightmarish night, and she knew that her father and sister would be worried. She told herself that there'd always be time later to get back to Gustav and whatever was bothering him. She even told herself that maybe he was just tired, and that she'd see him again soon, anyway. So she offered him a wave, which he returned, before she left the Gloom house alone. She crossed the overcast front lawn alone and opened the gate to take her first steps into a bright sunny day.

Of course, she wasn't alone for long, because as soon as she stepped outside the gate, her father and sister, who had been holding a sleepless vigil waiting for her, burst from their Fluorescent Salmon home and almost knocked her down, wrapping her in a tight, teary embrace.

Pearlie What hadn't taken a deep breath since beginning her own account of what she'd experienced the night before.

". . . so when I ran into the meeting, Dad was telling everybody, 'A neighborhood is not a place where every house looks the same as every other house! A neighborhood is a place where everybody takes care of one another and lets people be!' I walked in just in time to see people *cheer* him. Mrs. Everwiner looked like she'd just swallowed a big old plate of mud. They all voted her down *easily*!"

This was half an hour after Fernie's reunion with her family. They were all sitting around the dining room table, enjoying pancakes. Fernie had already provided her father and sister a breathless accounting of her night's adventures, and Pearlie was now doing the same for everything that had happened since the two sisters had seen each other last.

"So then I told Dad about October and about how you said we had to drive far away from here, and he was all, 'What? Well, we'll just see about that,' and he ran right back to the Gloom house, climbed the fence, and slammed his fists on the door, demanding to be let in, but of course the door wouldn't open, so he ran around the house looking for a way in, and. . ."

The way Pearlie told the story, Dad was a

hero; and Fernie had to agree that he was, even if he'd never really had a chance to actually do anything heroic.

But it was impossible to look at his glum expression, while Pearlie sang his praises.

It wasn't until breakfast was over and Pearlie ran to her bedroom to deal with some urgent business there that Fernie asked her father the big question, the one with the answer she was afraid she already knew. She said, "We're moving away, aren't we?"

Mr. What couldn't look at her. "Yes."

"But, Dad, none of it was his fault. He's my friend."

"I know he is," Mr. What said. "And I think he's a great kid. I like him as much as you do, and feel sorrier for him than I can ever say."

"If this is about my breaking your rules—"

"That's not the problem, honey. I know I told you never to go inside his house again, and that you disobeyed me by going, but there will always be times when I'm not around and you have to make judgments for yourself, even if that means doing things your nervous old nelly of a father considers too dangerous. You were clearly right about where you had to go in order to find help.

But you were only in danger because you lived here."

Fernie said, "The whole world was in danger from him, Dad. I wouldn't have been any safer from the monsters inside the Nightmare Vault if I'd been in Timbuktu or Antarctica or—what's that place—Liechtenstein."

"No, but you'd have been a little farther away from the danger, at least for a while. I'm sorry, Fernie. But we've only lived here a couple of weeks and you've already had to run for your life twice. So I'm afraid I'm going to have to start making arrangements to find another place to live, someplace *safer*, before something even more terrible happens. If I can help it, we'll be out of here before the school year starts."

Fernie stared at her father, loving him but also hating him; knowing he was right but also that he was wrong; knowing that he only wanted to protect her, and also knowing how much it hurt him to hurt her.

She was too afraid of what would come out of her mouth if she tried to argue, so she said, "May I be excused?"

He looked like his heart had broken. "Fernie, if you need to talk about this—"

"No," she said, knowing that he could not have felt worse if she'd thrown a tantrum and fought him. "It's okay. I understand. May I be excused?"

His shoulders slumped. "Yes, Fernie. Don't worry about the dishes. I'll clean up."

She took the dishes to the sink anyway, then went back to her room and closed the door, not coming out again for the rest of the day.

It wasn't until the next morning, when her father was busy on the phone talking to real estate agents, that Fernie slipped outside and stood beneath the bright light of the morning sun. She cast no shadow until her shadow, who she'd sent to tell Gustav she wanted to talk to him, flitted across the well-kept pavement of Sunnyside Terrace and returned to her, with the proud air of a spy who had just accomplished a dangerous mission.

Across the street, Gustav stood at the fence with a shape that she recognized as Great-Aunt Mellifluous, both waiting to see what she would do. She went to them, meeting them at the fence instead of circling around to the gate.

Behind the iron bars, wearing another of his identical little black suits, Gustav had never looked so imprisoned. "Hi."

Fernie's eyes burned. "Hi." She looked at Great-Aunt Mellifluous. "Hi."

"Hello, dear," Great-Aunt Mellifluous said. "I see that you've recovered from your ordeal. I know you sent for Gustav alone, but I wanted to apologize to you for not being there when you needed me; I wish I could have been with you throughout, but I had lots of hiding shadows to protect."

"And a little boy," Fernie was unable to resist saying, "who you didn't."

Great-Aunt Mellifluous drew back as if hurt, but nodded in acknowledgment that she deserved that much. "We'll talk later, dear. There are many things that need to be said."

She dissolved, like a creature of sugar who had just been doused with warm water, and joined the flowing gray mists at Gustav's feet.

He blinked at Fernie. "You're saying good-bye, right?"

She didn't ask him how he knew. She supposed he'd always known. He couldn't have been the boy he was, always looking out at the world through the iron bars of the Gloom estate fence, and not known that there would always be times when the strangeness he lived with drove potential friends away.

She could only tell him. "My dad says we're moving. Pearlie and I are both working on changing his mind."

"That's good," he said, without showing much faith that it would amount to anything. "I'm glad."

She closed her fists around the iron bars and squeezed them, as if just by wanting to she could twist them like pretzels, rip the fence down, and pull Gustav into the world with her. She looked away, warned herself not to cry, and then turned back to him with dry eyes. "But there's more, Gustav. I . . ."

"What?" he said.

"Gustav . . . I spent all day yesterday lying in my bed, thinking about everything that happened to us . . . and I think I've figured out what you wouldn't tell me. I know who became your mom after Penny died."

"Really?"

"It had to be someone who witnessed everything that happened inside the car when

October's shadows attacked. It had to be someone who was also able to take you from Penny and carry you away from the wreckage, alive, even though you hadn't even been born yet. It had to be someone who could keep you safe inside her until you were ready to be born, someone who could be your mother with Penny gone. It had to be someone who would do anything to protect you; someone your father would trust, whose story your father would believe; someone who would stay with you and raise you long enough to tell you what happened; someone who, just by being your mom until something happened to her, too, would make you what Hieronymus called you, a halfsie, half boy, half shadow. There's only one person I can think of who would fit all of that. Your mother was *the shadow of* the woman who *would have been* your mother. She was Penny's shadow, left behind after Penny died."

He said nothing.

Fernie went on: "That's the real reason you start evaporating if you ever walk outside the house's gates. It's not because you're like a vampire, burning up under the sun. That's what I thought when we first met, but there's a big ball of sunlight in your house and it doesn't bother you at all. No, you burn when you leave your property because only the shadow magic in your house can keep a halfsie boy alive."

He couldn't look at her.

Fernie waited until she couldn't stand the wait any longer and burst out, "Where's Penny's shadow, Gustav? What happened to her?"

"I don't know. She was just gone one day. But it must have been my fault. I know that much."

Fernie felt her cheeks growing hot. "What?"

"That's what I know, Fernie. That's what I've always known."

"I'm sorry, Gustav. But that's the single dumbest thing I've ever heard anybody say."

He seemed desperate for her to understand. "But if my parents hadn't been about to have me, they wouldn't have come back to this house. October wouldn't have become afraid of them deciding he couldn't stay. Penny wouldn't have died. My father wouldn't have gone after him, and wouldn't be a prisoner wherever he is now. I wouldn't be stuck here. All of that was my fault. Whatever happened to my shadow mom must have been my fault, too. Everything bad that's ever happened here was because of me."

He didn't cry, maybe because he'd already cried all he could over these thoughts, but he did seem to wilt a little, as if wanting to crumble into nothingness where he stood.

Fernie had only a second to act before he would have turned away and she would have lost him forever. So she reached through the bars, grabbed his wrists, and pulled him toward her.

"Don't you ever think that again," she said angrily. "You weren't even around when it all started and couldn't have done anything to stop it. Nothing that happened to your family was because of you. It was all October's fault. Everything bad that happened to your family was because of *him*."

His pale eyes turned wide and startled as he considered this really quite simple point for what may have been the first time in his short but very strange life.

She saw it sink in and become real to him.

They hugged through the bars until the front door of the What house opened and Fernie's father called her home.

ACKNOWLEDGMENTS

Repeating a theme from the first volume: You would not now be seeing this book without the persistence of agents extraordinaire Joshua Bilmes and Eddie Schneider of the Jabberwocky Literary Agency. You would not now be reading it in its present form without the input of the members of the South Florida Science Fiction Society Writers' Workshop, a group that includes Brad Aiken, Dave Dunn, Dave Slavin, and Chris Negelein. You would not now be enjoying the same experience free of verbal land mines and other clutter without the ace red pen of editor Jordan Hamessley and copy editors Kate Ritchey and Laura Stiers. You would not now be *ooh*ing and *aah*ing over the illustrations without the genius of artist Kristen Margiotta. You would not now be holding the divine artifact in your hands without designer Christina Quintero. You would not now be seeing any books from me at all without the patience, love, and constant encouragement of my beautiful wife, Judi B. Castro. You would not now be seeing a human being with my name and my face were it not for my parents, Saby and Joy Castro.

Also, just to keep matters interesting, you may have noticed that chapter 3 of this volume makes reference to a man who was once saved from freezing to death, by a pig. I wasn't kidding, people. That happened to me, at about age thirteen. So while we're thanking everybody, let's give a hearty thumbs-up to that pig.

ADAM-TROY CASTRO has said in interviews that he likes to jump genres and styles and has therefore refused to ever stay in place long enough to permit the unwanted existence of a creature that could be called a "typical" Adam-Troy Castro story. As a result, his short works range from the wild farce of his Vossoff and Nimmitz tales to the grim Nebula nominee "Of a Sweet Slow Dance in the Wake of Temporary Dogs." His twenty prior books include a nonfiction analysis of the Harry Potter phenomenon, four Spider-Man adventures, and three novels about his interstellar murder investigator, Andrea Cort (including a winner of the Philip K. Dick Award, *Emissaries from the Dead*). Adam's other award nominations include eight Nebulas, two Hugos, and three Stokers. Adam lives in Miami with his wife, Judi, and three insane cats named Uma Furman, Meow Farrow, and Harley Quinn.

KRISTEN MARGIOTTA attended the University of Delaware, where she majored in Visual Communications with a concentration in Illustration. Kristen received the Visual Communications Award for Excellence in Illustration, along with another colleague, during her final year at the university. When she graduated in 2005, Kristen began receiving commissions from buyers and selling her paintings. She also began exhibiting at regional galleries and events. In 2009, Kristen illustrated her first children's book, *Better Haunted Homes and Gardens*, and made her southwest gallery debut at the Pop Gallery in New Mexico. Her first NYC gallery exhibit was at the Animazing Gallery in 2012. Besides being an artist and illustrator, Kristen teaches at the Center for the Creative Arts in Yorklyn, Delaware, working with creative and exciting students who enjoy the arts.